KILLER WOMEN

Killer Women

Crime Club Anthology #1

Foreword by Val McDermid

TABLE OF CONTENTS

Foreword by Val McDermid   vii
1. The Window Man by Louise Millar   1
2. On the Undercliff by Alex Marwood   16
3. The Previous Tenant by Tammy Cohen   29
4. Schiaparelli Pink Bikini by Melanie McGrath   34
5. The Edge by Colette McBeth   49
6. The Rat Trap by Jane Casey   57
7. Don't Know Where, Don't Know When by Erin Kelly   68
8. *El Llorón Borrego* by Sarah Hilary   82
9. Stop the Pigeon by Louise Voss   89
10. The Day of the Dead by Alison Joseph   109
11. The Secret Ingredient by Helen Smith   128
12. Witch by Kate Medina   148
13. Stevie by D.E. Meredith   153
14. Chance by Laura Wilson   163
15. Natural Justice by Kate Rhodes   180
Author Biographies   187

FOREWORD

VAL MCDERMID

Whenever I am confronted by an anthology of killer short stories, I always feel like Little Jack Horner. I can't wait to stick in my thumb and pull out a plum. I love the variety that comes with a selection box of short stories; there's so much to love, so much to surprise me, and if I don't like one or two quite so much, well, it's not like I've made too much of a commitment.

It's also the perfect route to discover new writers. This Killer Women anthology introduced me to fresh and startling aspects of writers I thought I knew, and to others whose work I've been meaning to read but hadn't got to yet. I'll be putting that right now...

The short story has been a feature of the crime genre since the very beginning. Writers were often commissioned by newspapers and magazines to provide short entertainments for readers who didn't have enough time to read novels but craved the satisfactions of fiction. Because so many of their readers were women, those magazines often commissioned women writers to provide those entertaining squibs of short fiction. And still they're the perfect accompaniment to those small morsels of time that crop up in our busy schedules.

For writers there is as much delight in the short form as there is for readers. Sometimes we have a neat little idea that could never sustain a novel. Sometimes a disturbing voice creeps into our heads that we would quite like to play with but not for as long as it takes to write a book. Sometimes we just want a complete break from our series characters, to show we're not just one-trick ponies.

For anyone who has succumbed to the notion that women are the gentler sex, this collection will make your head spin. There is darkness, there is suspense, there is horror and danger. But there is also exuberance, humour and moments of wry recognition.

So whether you're on a train or a bus, whether you're in a queue or the loo, whether you're unwinding in bed or in a bar, take a Killer Woman with you. I promise you won't be disappointed.

THE WINDOW MAN

LOUISE MILLAR

The broken glass was scattered over the floor. Sarah found a broom and swept it up, shivering in the wintry breeze blowing in the smashed window. Under the kitchen spotlights, the tiniest fragments shone, stuck in the tile grooves. She dabbed at them with a wet kitchen towel so that they didn't end up in someone's foot.

Where was he?

The kitchen clock said 5.57 p.m.

If he didn't come soon, she'd have to locate the toolbox and board this up. She looked through the jagged hole to see if there was a shed somewhere out in the dark garden. Something banged in the wind. A dustbin or gate, maybe.

Socks barked, making her jump. A beam danced around the walls of the hallway as a car triggered the security light in the front driveway.

'Good boy,' Sarah said, switching on lamps as she followed him down the hallway to the window.

A van was drawing up outside, '24-hour Emergency Glaziers' written on the side.

The driver climbed out. His thin body seemed to unfold as he stood up, and he surveyed the upstairs windows of the cottage. She guessed that being tall was useful for his work.

and Ro had left. Watch some telly. Have a glass of wine to take the edge off.

'So what are you, then – a house-sitter?' the window man called through, unhurried, examining the broken glass under the spotlight.

She dabbed buttons on her phone. 'Well, dog-sitter, really.'

'How's that work, then? You with an agency?'

'No, no. I'm friends with the owner. Ro. We work together. I'm just doing it as a favour.'

'Chance to get away from the husband and kids for a few nights, eh?' he said, winking.

He *was* flirting. She returned to the kitchen, wrapping her oversize cardigan around her to remind him that it was freezing.

'So can you do this tonight?'

'Depends.' He put the tape measure away.

'On what?'

'Want it toughened?'

'Sorry?'

'The glass. That's toughened glass in there.' He pointed at the jagged mess around the frame. 'Harder to break.' He leaned outside. 'Look, there you go. Little bastards used a brick.'

'Is it?' This was getting complicated. 'Does that cost extra?'

He whistled. 'Add a hundred?'

'I'll need to ask Ro. Let me see if she's there yet.' She tapped at her phone again.

'So if you're not a professional dog-sitter, what are you?' he said, leaning back on the worktop.

'Teacher.'

His eyes grew wider. 'Hang on. Your mate's a teacher and she lives round here? Good grief. What are they paying you lot these days?'

Sarah kept her eyes on the screen. '*She's* a teacher. *He's* a doctor.'

He grinned and folded his arms. 'You lot never liked me.'

'What, teachers?'

'Got excluded twice.' There was pride in his voice. She knew she was supposed to ask why.

She held out her blank screen. 'Right. Still no reply. I think we'll just go with toughened. But could you do it quick? I've got to go out tonight,' she lied.

'I can.' He picked up his bag and headed to the front door, taking in the tasteful landscape paintings and elegant lamps. 'Give me an hour.'

'An hour?' she said, following him.

'Got to go back to the shop.'

'Can't you do it now, in your van?'

'Not if it's toughened.'

The temptation to tell him to use any glass was overwhelming. But then she wouldn't be able to relax in case it was the wrong decision. 'Well, if it's an hour, OK.'

He gave her a quizzical glance. 'Thought you had to go out?'

'I can delay it.'

He turned at the front door and looked back up the dark staircase. 'They check the house for you, the Old Bill?'

'Yes,' she lied again. 'It was all fine. Right, so see you in an hour?'

'Two hours.'

'Sorry?'

'Take me half an hour to get back to the shop. An hour to do it. Half an hour back.' He pointed at the antique grandfather clock ticking loudly in the hall. 'About eight, probably. You can get the kettle on. If I'm not stopping you from going out, that is.'

The joke in his voice told her he wasn't stupid.
Resigned, she let him out.

Turning off the hall lights again as the van drove away, Sarah picked up Socks and headed up the winding cottage stairs. They creaked in protest. Socks raced off at the top, sniffing corners.

There were three bedrooms. She started in the spare room, where she was sleeping. It was the smaller of the doubles, the plaster artfully worked around the seventeenth-century walls and ceiling beams so that it looked both period and contemporary. The bed was made up with crisp white cotton. A red velvet chair added what she believed was called an 'accent colour'.

James and Ro wouldn't mind her looking around, not in the circumstances.

She opened the wardrobe and found what she suspected were their overflow clothes. The cottage might sit in an affluent part of the London commuter belt, but it was small, even though she guessed its price tag wasn't.

These must be Ro's smart clothes. At school she wore no-nonsense smart black or tan trousers, with a range of shirts. The ones here were expensive and feminine: evening dresses and trouser suits, in silks and soft jersey. Sarah imagined Ro dressed up in them for functions with James, sitting at dinner parties with their doctor friends.

Nobody – family or friends – had asked her out anywhere since Ian had left. What would they even say to her?

A red Jaeger dress hung in a dry-cleaning slip. She took it out and pushed an arm through the sleeve. It was size 8. Her old size. Her arm stuck halfway.

Ian wouldn't recognise her any more.

Next she checked under the spare bed. There were taste-ful wooden storage boxes. One held Ro's summer shoes; another had photo albums.

She took one out to flick through it.

It belonged to James. It was from a time before he met Ro. He was young in the photos, a teenager and a student. His hair was still dark, but not short and groomed like today, but in an '80s flat-top. He was abroad somewhere, one of a group of teenage boys. He was wearing a white shirt open at the neck, showing off a deep tan. In another, he was wearing a sleeveless white vest that displayed the muscled, tanned arms of a fit young man. His blue eyes sparkled with freedom.

She wondered when James and Ro had met.

What had made them decide to build a life together.

That choice you make.

The trust that takes.

Sarah moved on to the smallest bedroom, which James used as a study. His medical degrees adorned the wall. It struck her as a strange thing, to put up your professional achieve-ments on the wall. Ro must have hung them for him. James seemed too kind and considerate a man to do something so vain.

Last, she checked their bedroom. You had to duck through a low doorway and go down old stairs into a large carpeted room, with more beams, a French-style bed made up with more white cotton, and a bronze freestanding bath in the middle. An uncurtained window overlooked what she guessed, in the dark, were fields.

Sarah sat beside the bath and imagined them in here, Ro in the bath, dark shiny hair piled on her head, James in this chair, asking about her day. Him announcing the exciting news that he'd been invited to a conference in San Francisco and had swung it that she could go with him.

She stood up and checked inside the main wardrobes. Ro's work clothes hung there. Jackets that she recognised as James's.

She returned to the hall.

Three bedrooms.

She guessed they couldn't have kids or didn't want to. Either way, this way of living seemed to suit them. Everything had a place. Everything fitted together.

It was chilly, so she went downstairs to the boiler and read the instructions stuck inside the door. She took a photo with her phone so she could put the controls back the way they wanted them, before turning it on to 'full', then found the oven switch and photographed that too before turning it on. She fed Socks and let him out in the garden, trying to ignore the gaping hole in the window, and cooked her dinner, eating it in front of the log fire.

When the window man drove into the driveway around eight, she put her mobile to her ear.

'Hi,' she mouthed as he entered. 'I'm just on the phone to my sister. Are you OK to go ahead?'

'Yup.' He looked unconvinced.

She sat on the sofa and pretended she was discussing a tricky student with Gemma, watching the glazier repairing the glass in the reflection of the TV.

Fifteen minutes later, he coughed and handed her an invoice.

'Hang on, Gemma,' Sarah said, pressing the phone into her chest. 'Thanks,' she said, taking it and walking to the front door.

'I was telling my mate about this gang you were telling me about,' the window man said as she opened it for him to leave. 'Says they poured oil in a swimming pool next village along.'

'No!' She opened her eyes wide. 'That's terrible. Well, listen, thanks. I'll pop by with the cash tomorrow.'

She recognised defeat in the slope of his shoulders, but there was nothing she could do about it.

As he drove off, she walked into the kitchen and stood at the freshly installed toughened glass, looking out into the dark garden, wondering what Gemma would say if she did ring.

That night, Sarah couldn't sleep. Without Ian, it had become impossible.

A shed door banged somewhere down at the far end of the garden.

She lay on the spare bed and watched the branches of tall trees waving outside the window.

Restless, she got up and wandered into James and Ro's bedroom and turned on a lamp.

A wedding photo sat on the beside table.

She picked it up and examined James's eyes, still as blue as in the teenage photos but now with soft crinkles around them. He had kind eyes. Thoughtful eyes. Eyes that made you feel he could see inside your head. Eyes that made you feel understood.

She'd told no one, because they'd think she was mad, but the last few times she'd met James, she'd seen an intensity in them when he looked at her, almost as if he were trying to communicate something.

She sat on the bed, wondering what it would be like to be Ro, to have a husband so comfortable in himself that he could give so easily to others. Sarah saw Ro at the school gate sometimes, chatting to parents with an effortless calm confidence, and she guessed that living with James must help you be like that.

Sarah lay down on the white cotton duvet and turned off the lamp.

Ian used to sleep behind her, curled up into her body, hand on her tummy. Now there was just cold air. She couldn't sleep with just cold air.

For a moment, she imagined being Ro instead, lying here, James's comforting hand on her stomach.

And before she knew it, she had finally fallen asleep.

A creak woke her. She opened her eyes. The lamp was still on.

A second loud creak sounded in the hallway.

'Socks?' she whispered. He snuffled at the bottom of the bed.

The creaks had come from the stairs.

Enveloped in a cold sweat, Sarah rolled off the bed and dropped to the floor, crawled over and hid behind the door.

Was somebody here?

Had James and Ro come home?

Holding her breath, she peered around the door and down the stairs into a hall full of shadows.

The grandfather clock ticked on.

At her back she felt the faint heat of a radiator and realised it had been cooling down.

Another loud creak came from the hall radiator.

The central heating.

Shivering, she stood up and returned to James and Ro's bedroom and sat at the dressing table, rubbing her puffy eyes in the mirror. A polished wooden box caught her eye.

She opened it and pulled out a bundle of cards.

They were Valentine cards from James and Ro to each other.

Twenty-two of them, she counted, the date marked on each one. They varied from jokey messages to each other that pretended to disguise the identity of the sender to flowery declarations of love.

She counted and checked, noticing something odd.

The cards from 2010 were missing.

Did they split up?

Did Ro have an affair?

It certainly wouldn't have been James.

Sarah's eyes travelled to a pair of silver scissors beside the box.

The week in James and Ro's house passed fast. Unable to sleep each night, Sarah felt increasingly unwell and on the second day rang in sick. She'd been doing that a lot recently, and she sensed an impatience in her boss's voice that made sleeping even more difficult. Each day she walked Socks around the fields, and at night she found herself back in the kitchen, looking out at the dark garden through the toughened window, thinking about how things had come to this.

The day before Ro and James were due back, she washed the sheets, cleaned the cottage and, using the photos she'd taken, returned the switches and boiler to the previous settings and double-locked the front door behind her, as she had found it.

On the doorstep, she looked at the spare keys in her hand. She couldn't just post them back through the letterbox to lie on the hall floor – not with burglars in the area.

She'd have to keep them and give them back in person.

The thought of seeing James soon made everything feel better.

The flat was in a state when she returned home to Guildford. Her housemates had not washed up, and the despair returned of living back in a cheap student share after five years in her beautiful, immaculate newbuild home with Ian. She waited in her bedroom till everyone had gone out, then locked herself in the bathroom and dyed her hair back from blonde to brown, put her glasses back on and took off the heels that made her taller. She felt like herself again.

She really didn't feel well, however, so she took two more days off work, reassuring her boss by phone that she would see the doctor this week and talk about increasing her medication.

That Thursday, she arrived at the clinic at 1.50 p.m., nice and early.

'Dr Rainyard at two,' she told the receptionist.

She sat in the waiting room, the anxiety growing that he wouldn't be here, that he'd have been called away on an emergency.

But the door opened on time, and he waved her into his office with a welcoming smile.

'How was your holiday?' Sarah asked as they sat down in his office.

'Good, thanks,' he replied. 'And how've you been?'

'I've been away myself, actually.'

'Have you?' He nodded in appreciation. 'When we spoke last time, you said you were worried about going on holiday on your own. You talked about how it would be the first holiday since Ian.'

She held up a thumb. 'But I did it.'

'And how was it?'

'It was fine,' she replied. 'I was surprised. I house-sat for a friend at work. I walked a lot, slept a lot. I was fine. Even though someone tried to break in.'

'When you were in the house?' He looked alarmed.

'No. Just before I arrived.'

'That must have been frightening.'

She held out her open palms like he did. 'It was OK, actually. I coped. I called the police and the window man. But what worries me is that I found myself going through my friend's things while I was there. And her husband's. I feel quite bad about it. I went through everything. I opened their letters, their drawers, their bills. I couldn't stop.'

She watched his expression. Nothing changed. She began to relax.

As was normal, they began to discuss her trust issues. About how Ian had left her for her sister, and the baby they had had that was supposed to be hers.

The hour passed quickly. It always did.

'So did you go anywhere nice?' Sarah said, pulling on her coat at 3 p.m.

'No, no. I was just gardening, catching up.'

She stood up. 'You always say that.'

'What?'

'That you never go away.'

'Well, is it important where I am?'

'No,' she replied, 'but it feels strange sometimes. I've been coming here for two years, and I always ask you where you went on holiday, and you always say, "I didn't – I just caught up with the gardening." I think you're not telling me the truth.'

He frowned. 'Why is it important that you know where I am, Sarah? What do you think will happen to you if I'm not here?'

She ignored his question. 'What's important is that I come here to discuss my issues around betrayal and trust, but you lie to me too. I think you don't tell me where you go on holiday, in the same way that you never speak to me about your personal life. I don't know anything about where you live. Or whether you have a family. I don't even know how old you are.'

He sat back. 'Why do you think that's important for me to do that?'

Sarah shrugged. 'I think it's part of your training. It's about creating boundaries so I don't form an unhealthy attachment to you. So I feel safe in here.'

That intense look entered his eye, the one that told her he was trying to communicate something but couldn't. 'OK, well, listen, time's up for today. But what you've said is very interesting. Let's pick up there next time.'

'OK,' she said, walking to the door and waiting for him to open it for her.

On the back of the door hung a jacket.

As James opened the door, she slipped the spare front door keys she'd found in his hall drawer into the pocket and pushed them down into the hole she'd made with Ro's silver scissors. Sometime soon, the mystery of the missing spare keys would be solved and forgotten.

Sarah said goodbye and headed off.

If she was quick, she'd have time to reach Ro's school for pickup time and watch her chatting to parents for a while, before heading home before Socks got lonely on his own back in the flat.

Tomorrow she'd take another day off work and return to the Internet to find out more about Ro, perhaps try to track down some of her local Facebook friends in person and befriend them, and discover what happened back in

2010 and what Ro did to James. It must have been something bad. She just knew it.

When James looked at her like he did today, she knew now she was right; he was telling her that he wanted her, like she wanted him, but that Ro was in the way.

Next time she saw on the Internet that James was due at a medical conference abroad, she might pay Ro a visit at the cottage.

It didn't matter about the spare keys. Sarah didn't need them anyway.

She could just break the window again.

ON THE UNDERCLIFF

ALEX MARWOOD

'This *has* to be it,' he says.

'I don't see why,' she replies. 'Every other road on Malta looks exactly the same, as far as I can see.'

They study the narrow opening hacked through the living rock that heads straight for the cliff edge from the single-track road on which they're parked. Someone has been at the golden stone with a pot of red paint. '*TIDHOLX*' says the wall on her right. Keep out. '*PRIVAT*' bellows the other. Not exactly welcoming.

'Yes, but,' he says, 'every other road isn't pointing downhill off this one, is it?'

'I'm not sure we should.' She peers down the track. It drops at what looks like a forty-five-degree incline between great stone slab walls. Those walls have come from a temple, she thinks. Vincent Micallef says that there were several more scattered across the Maltese archipelago, but they were dismantled over the millennia to make walls or simply reburied when found by scratch farmers unwilling to give their limited land up to a government that would seize it at a sneeze of historical tourism. You can't blame them, really. 'It's very steep.'

'You were the one who wanted to go off the beaten track,' he says. Flourishing the map at her, he stabs a finger at the clearly marked '*tempil*' between the cliff on which they sit and the sea. 'I was perfectly happy to go to the ones everyone else goes to. It was you who was going on about the romance being ruined by the EU tents and the ticket offices.'

'I...' she says. 'Yes, but this looks really rough. I don't know if we'll even clear some of those ridges in the track. What if we get stuck down there?'

'We'll find someone to pull us out.'

'Who?'

'Well, I don't know, do I? Someone. There's always someone, in the end.'

The temperature must top forty degrees in the midday sun. Locked in this sardine-tin Fiat, even with the air-con eating away at the petrol gauge, they had long since retreated into ill-tempered adolescent snarls.

'On this road? Come on, Harry. You know Vincent says it's practically deserted up here. And he says that there are still troglodytes living on this side of the island, and they don't like outsiders much.'

Harry treats her to one of his explosions of mocking laughter. His twelfth today, by her count. She started counting on Monday, and now it's Thursday and the total is nearing triple digits. Rose grinds her teeth. *Why?* she asks herself again. *Why did I agree to two whole weeks, when we've never been on holiday together before?* They say you never really know someone until you travel with them, and that's certainly true in this case.

'Ha! Troglodytes?' He guffaws. 'I suppose they're lurking behind the rocks with their clubs and animal skins!'

Rose blinks. 'I didn't say that.'

'Oh yes, you did.' He has, she's noticed, a habit of direct contradiction. A habit that she's concluded, since social media has laid open so many of the faults in human thinking en masse to those interested in observing them, is common among people who know less than they believe they do. Henry believes that all words mean what he understands them to mean, and only that. His world is one without subtlety, without nuance, and without all but the most basic of puns. *It's my own fault,* she thinks. *If I hadn't been so busy projecting in the hope of finding someone nice, I would have noticed.*

'It just means they live in caves,' she protests. 'They're hardly the only –'

'Cavemen. Precisely,' says Harry, and swings the car into the narrow lane before she can object any further. 'Well, we've come all this way in this heat, so I vote we do what we came for. Did you *really* think that there was a tribe of Neolithic hunters living on an island that's thirty miles by twenty in the twenty-first century without having anthropologists swarming over them?'

Rose sighs. 'I didn't *say* that, Harry.'

'Yes, you did,' he assures her, and drops down into second gear to slow their progress down the ravine. Rose experiences a surge of white-hot rage so intense that she almost raises her hand and punches him in the side of his head. But good sense and civilisation hold her back. *And then what?* she asks herself. *These walls are so close to the sides of the car there's no way I'm getting the door open more than a few inches. I'd be trapped in this boiling-hot tin box with an angry man whose blood pressure hovers on the edge of dangerous at the best of times. His head would explode, and then I'd be stuck in here, slowly dying of thirst with a melting corpse until eventually someone finds our skeletons when they come down to harvest the caper berries in the autumn...*

She counts to ten, breathing in through her nose and out through her mouth. *It's OK,* she tells herself. *Six more days and we're done. I'll collect my bags from the belt, tell him at the airport, and catch a cab home while he goes to collect his car from the car park.* Nothing lost but two weeks and a few months of fooling myself. It's one of the things they don't tell you about getting older. There's a band between the divorce zone and the funeral zone where basically all the men on the market are the arseholes that other women didn't want. *I'm better off alone while I'm passing through it.*

'I was just saying,' she says as calmly as she can, 'that Vincent Micaleff says that the people down here don't like outsiders. Didn't you see the sign? The PRIVAT? And that graffiti up on the plain about the holiday homes?' She suppresses an inward suck of breath as the left-hand wing mirror catches on a jag of protruding rock and flips inwards. If they get out of this with their insurance excess intact, it will be a miracle.

'Oh, good grief, woman.' Harry opens his window to fold his own mirror in against the car, and a rush of air hot enough to cook bread bursts through the air conditioning. Neither of them had really taken in before they came how much more North Africa Malta is than Europe. Lulled by photos of rococo interiors, she had imagined a sea-encircled Tuscany with avenues of cypresses to shade the way. This seared desert rock, with its walls and stairs and domes and minaret-like church towers, is beautiful, no question, but it's a harsh, forbidding landscape. The generations that grew up here, through siege and famine, overrun by invader after invader, building temples and burying them, must have a core of granite in their very souls.

He closes the window. Treats her to a gaze of smirking patronage. 'Dear girl,' he says (*When did you start calling me that?* she wonders. *I'm in my forties. I run the English department at a thousand-pupil school. When did I become a girl again?*), 'you really have to stop believing everything anyone tells you just because they're a local. Of course Vincent Micaleff would say that. He wants you to stay in Marsascala, spending money in his restaurant, not gadding off spending it elsewhere.'

'Oh, please. So how come it was him who sent us to Tarxien? And Valletta? And that restaurant in the marina at Ta' Xbiex?'

Harry snorts. 'Yes, well, they're probably all cousins of his or something.'

It's only during this trip that she's become fully aware of Harry's damning attitude to foreigners. Is he a racist? Is it as bad as that? Or is it just a generalised fear of the unfamiliar? Either way, it frustrates the hell out of her. Every single tip she's picked up from chatting with the locals has been greeted with grudging suspicion at the very best.

He takes his foot off the brake and allows the car to trickle forward under its own weight. There's a corner fifty yards ahead. God knows what's beyond, but anything has to be better than this stifling limestone canyon. 'And besides,' he continues, 'surely you've noticed that they're all suspicious of anywhere that's not where they live? I've never met such a provincial mindset. Honestly, they make our North-South divide look positively sophisticated. Mention any town you're not in right now to a local and their first response is to suck air in through their teeth.'

'Oh, please,' says Rose. 'Like they don't do that everywhere in the world.'

'Not in *my* world,' he says.

'How marvellous,' says Rose. 'I shall very much look forward to going to Liverpool for our next trip, then.'

Harry sucks air through his teeth.

They reach the corner in silence. *I actually dislike you, Harry*, she thinks. *That's what's happened these last few days.*

I've gone from uncertainty to active dislike. And now he's driving me down this hill, and God knows how we're going to get back up it again. We're in a Fiat Uno, not a four-by-four. We'll get stuck at the bottom of this track and we'll have to find someone to pull us out with a tractor or something. If they can even get a tractor down here.

'And anyway,' he says, 'they always hide the best swimming places to stop the tourists getting to them. Keep them to themselves. I mean. St Peter's Pool wasn't signed at *all*, was it?'

'Yes, but people were perfectly happy to tell us how to get there.'

'Whatever,' he says. 'I promise you, we'll get down to the bottom and there'll be a marvellous little cove with hardly anybody there.'

She doesn't reply. Rose can be a sulker, she knows that, but it doesn't mean that she has any great control over the sulk when it comes upon her.

'Oh, sorry,' says Harry, 'I forgot. We'll have to fight our way through the *cavemen* first.'

She leans forward and fiddles pointedly with the air-con dial.

'Do you think they'll be cannibals, as well?' he asks.

Rose rolls her eyes. 'Just shut up, Harry. It's not funny. Just because you didn't know about it doesn't mean it's not a thing.'

'Only joking,' he says, in that voice that makes her eyeballs bulge.

'Well, don't.'

At the corner, the track flattens out and widens. Just enough to allow a vehicle to make the turn, not enough to allow it to turn right round. Another *TIDHOLX*, smeared in scarlet paint, runs the length of the turn. 'They really don't want us down here,' she says.

'Well, tough,' he replies. 'It's not like we have much alternative now, is it?'

'Well, we *did*,' she says, and eyes the road ahead. Still just the one lane, walls lower now, so she can see the tiny patchwork fields surprisingly much closer than when she last saw them. The undercliff is deserted. It looks as though it has been so for many years. The little fields are overrun and the terrace walls are sagging. And there is no one here. Not a figure to be seen on the baking plain, and the little one-room farmhouses – rooms, as they're known locally – are collapsing. The road drops slowly down the face of the cliff, a shelf carved out, God knows how, to carry them down to the valley. She glimpses the plain and sees that it is scattered with tiny rock cairns. *I know what those are*, she thinks. Up on the clifftop she sees a figure silhouetted against the azure sky. Oh, thank God, she thinks. There *are* people up here, at least on the proper road. The figure stands and gazes down at them, then raises one arm and gestures towards the great headland that cuts them off from the beach at Ghajn Tuffieha. *Should I tell him?* she wonders. Decides not. He'll probably resent the implication that he doesn't know what he's doing.

She points out the cairns, in the hope that they can make the squabble blow over. 'They use them for blowing tiny songbirds out of the sky during the migration season.'

'Or maybe,' he says, 'they use them to offer up the innards of their human sacrifices to the sun god,' and sniggers.

Rolling her eyes, she cranes to see the drop as they pass a spot where the wall has gone entirely and left a gap, and shrinks back into the car. 'Jesus. Oh, good God, Harry, why did you bring us down here?'

He can't see from his side. 'What?'

'Stop. Just stop the car and get out and look.'

Harry pulls over to the left and gets out. Walks past the front of the car, leaving the door open to let out the cool, and looks down at what she's seen. Buried in a forest of prickly pear, sandwiched between boulders the size of bungalows, stubby trees growing up through wheel shafts and shattered windscreens, is a small collection of shattered cars. A minibus, snapped clean in half. A four-by-four, white paint covered in rust and canvas canopy ripped and bleached and spread across a rock. The remains of a Hillman Imp, barely showing through the mat of capers that pours over its caved-in sides. Rose winds down the window and listens to the distant shush of the sea. Has a horrible vision of herself, teeth bared and screaming as their back wheels lose purchase on the dusty ground. *This lane is probably a flash-flood route,* she thinks nonsensically beneath the cloudless sky. *I hate this. We're in trouble, I know we're in trouble, and he's just sucking his teeth and scratching his arse.*

'It's just a car dump,' he says. 'You know what they're like. They've shoved them over the edge to save on scrappage.'

'How do you *know* that?' she asks. His assumptions are turning her purple with frustration. 'How can you be so *sure*?'

Harry sighs and comes back to the driver's side. 'Come on,' he says. 'Half the walls are made of empty oil drums up in these rural bits, and the rest is old fridges. It's what they do. And besides, how are we going to get through that wall at ten miles an hour?'

'I...We have no idea how stable this track is. For all we know...'

'Or perhaps,' he says, because he can never let a chance to snipe lie when he sees it, 'it's the cars of all their previous victims. Once they've done away with them and gnawed their bones.'

'Oh, shut up.' Rose closes her eyes and grips the door handle. He puts the car back into gear.

DANGER says the red paint at the next corner, as the road finally reaches the plain. *NO ENTRY.*

'I just love the way they keep on with this,' says Harry, 'as though we had a choice.'

Rose wants to scream, WE HAD A CHOICE! She wants to shout in his face, cover him with spittle, and smack that smug mouth till it bleeds. *But you took it away from us right up at the top of that cliff with your unilateral strike. Let me out! I'll walk back up to the top and find a bus. Or hitchhike. Anything rather than be stuck in here with you. Come on. I don't want to be here. Let me out!*

But she stays silent. Harry manoeuvres his way around the hairpin, and the undercliff opens up in front of them. A long way from the beachside idyll he promised at the top. It's obvious from the moment they emerge that they are much further above sea level than they had imagined: that instead of an easy rock scramble from the edge of a field to the sea, the plain ends in another dizzying drop into the glutinous suck of deep black water. *Kraken territory*, she thinks. *I doubt anyone has swum from this piece of coastline since time began.*

And the fields. They clearly were fields once, but it looks as though whoever farmed them gave up long ago. The topsoil must be millimetres thin here, carried away over the cliff by winter winds. All that grows here now are stunted oleanders, caper bushes, tangles of dried-out wild fennel and great forests of prickly pear. The bleached tomato fields in the central plain below Mdina look lush and fruitful by comparison. But at least there are fields now, which must mean field entrances. Somewhere along this track they must come across an opportunity to turn round.

They creep along the road in the desert light, bumping and sliding where the cart ruts – *how can you wear cart ruts in solid stone?* – go suddenly deep and catch the car's underside with great bangs and shrieks of scraping metal. *It has to finish in a turnabout*, thinks Rose. *It's not possible for it to simply peter out.* She glances up to look for the man on the clifftop. He's still there. One arm pointing left, the other working like a windmill. *How funny*, she thinks. *That looks like semaphore. I'd swear it was.*

The dazzle becomes too much. Her eyes drift down the limestone rock face. For a moment it is all white-gold uniformity; then her eyes adjust and she sees that there are, indeed, as their landlord told her yesterday evening, caves in the face of it. Dark breaks in the stone, many out of reach of anything but the seabirds, but lower, where land slopes up to meet cliff, a whole network of them partially hidden behind rudimentary walls.

'There!' she cries. 'Harry! You see?'

He grinds to a halt and looks in the direction of her pointing finger. 'Livestock shelters.'

You can never admit you're wrong, can you? she thinks.

'You didn't really think those were houses, did you?' he asks. 'Nobody lives in caves. Are you nuts? And besides, even if they did, they've probably been abandoned for years. Where would their kids go to school, for God's sake? Where would they get their food?'

'I don't know,' she says. 'God, why do you think I have all the answers?'

They fall silent for a moment. Then: 'Heh,' says Harry, 'they're probably lighting the cooking fires right now,' and waggles his fingers at her like Vincent Price.

And she laughs. It's silly, all this bad temper because the day is hot and they've lost their way. Slaps his shoulder, half in reproof, half in fondness. *I shouldn't have left the cool-bag in the boot,* she thinks. *We should have been keeping our fluids up. No wonder we're tetchy. When we reach the end, I'll get it out and we can have a nice big drink of water and a pastizz, and everything will look better.*

'Oi, oi,' says Harry, and slows down once more. Ahead, the road divides neatly around another curved wall, another message daubed on it in the blood-red paint. An arrow, pointing right, and a single word:

TEMPIL.

'Well!' he says. 'There you go! I told you!'

She feels her spirits soar. Not so much, any more, at the thought of seeing the special site alone, while the tourists swarm over Hagar Qim with their ice creams, but at the simple knowledge that, if there's a temple, there *must* be clear ground around it. And with clear ground, there *must* be space to turn around at last.

'Oh, thank God for that!' she cries. Harry guns the engine and swings in the direction the arrow points. The walls close round them once again, sharp edges inches from her window and the heat so strong that even the air-con can no longer fight it off. She feels sweat begin to trickle from her hairline. But she no longer cares. The water in the boot will still be cool, for it was solid ice when she put it in.

'So funny,' she says. 'I've suddenly realised what this reminds me of. This road.'

'What's that?' he asks.

'When I was a kid,' she says, 'on my uncle's farm in Wales. They had a run like this leading to the sheep dip. It was sort of like a funnel. Got narrower and narrower the further you went in, with high walls and then fences, so that eventually the sheep could only go one by one, and the only way out was through the dip. Like that. That's what this reminds me of.'

Harry laughs. 'Gawd,' he says. 'Like a slaughterhouse. You're as bad as me. You'll be giving yourself the willies again.'

Ahead, a gateway. Great slabs again, replacing the drystone.

Harry stops, looking at it in open-mouthed wonder. 'My God. This is the *actual* temple entrance! No car park or anything – we get to actually drive straight in!'

'Wow,' she says. 'Amazing. Better not let the EU get wind of this.'

They drive through, park up, get out.

'My God,' says Rose, 'it's perfect.' Tucks her hand around his arm and squeezes, does a little wiggle of excitement. 'It's *perfect!*'

The temple is small, but looks untouched since the Neolithic. The ones they have seen so far have all been broken, fragmented, roped off to keep straying hands from touching what remains of the weathered rock. Sunk ten feet down into a virtual bullring, this little sacred place slumbers in the afternoon light as though the priests have simply gone for a siesta. It looks as though it's been assembled, the fingertip polka-dot patterns, the swirling sun motifs, by hands that are still alive. They walk forward, transported. 'My God, it even has a roof!' she says. 'I don't believe it! Why does nobody know about this? How do we get it all to ourselves?'

'I guess people have just...forgotten about it,' he says. 'When the cave people went away. It's like we've fallen off the edge of the world.'

'How could they leave?' she asks. 'How? If you lived somewhere like this, would you ever leave? I mean, I know it must be a hard life, but... oh my goodness, Harry! Look at this! There's even still paint! On the altar! They *said* at Hagar Qim that they were probably decorated with paint, but...'

Harry goes over to examine the deep rust pigment more closely. It's definitely a stain of some sort, clearly different from the golden Malta stone. It's almost Georgian in its richness. Who'd have thought the Neolithic people could have made a shade so vibrant that it's still, after all these millennia, this rich, rusty shade of...

Oxblood.

Beside him, a head and shoulders pop up over a stone as if from nowhere. Then another behind Rose's head. And another and another until the temple is encircled. Small people, their hair cut shaggily as though with a flint knife.

No one speaks.

THE PREVIOUS TENANT

TAMMY COHEN

Abby arranges her collection of miniature cacti on the windowsill where once, according to www.mostdisgustingcrimes.com, five fat human hearts sat in a row as if keeping watch over the street outside. She shouldn't have looked on those websites. Doesn't know how she'll ever sleep now she knows exactly what happened here. Where he kept them. What he did to them. One site even has a helpful annotated diagram of the layout of the flat, with brief descriptions of what he did and arrows pointing to each spot. She had to move the Moroccan pouffe after she saw it.

'Is it my imagination, or does it feel chilly in here?' she asks.

Charlie, hunched over his laptop at the table a few feet away, doesn't reply, so she opens the window and holds out her hand.

'Yep. Definitely colder in here than outside.'

She's not really interested in the weather. What she really wants to ask is why she ever allowed him to talk her into this. What she really wants to know is why he never listens to her, why her opinion doesn't count. But she doesn't want to start a row. Not on moving-in day. Not when this is supposed to be a new start. Not when, as he keeps saying, he's doing it for her.

'Done it!'

Charlie makes that air-punch gesture he does when Arsenal scores or he kills someone in *Call of Duty*.

'It's all up on the site. Listen to this: "Making a programme about the Pilchard Street murders? Now you have the chance to film in the very place where the gruesome killings took place. Email to get our exclusive daily rates." People like that, don't they, when you tell them something's exclusive?'

'I guess, but –'

'Hang on, there's more: "Or maybe you just fancy having a photograph taken in the living room where Francis Downham first brought his victims, or on the bed where he kept them bound and gagged for days on end, or posing in the bath where he dismembered the bodies. For a flat fee of £75 you can grab yourself a slice of living history." Do you see what I did with that word *slice*? What do you think? It's good, right?'

It's something Charlie does a lot. Answer his own questions, as if she is not really necessary to the interaction. As if she might just as well not exist at all.

'Well, technically it's not the *actual* bed, is it? They got rid of all the furniture afterwards; that's what that agent told us. "Totally refurbished from top to bottom," he said. Anyway, I just think it'll be a bit weird, having a load of strangers tramping around our flat.'

Abby doesn't look at Charlie when she speaks, addressing her words to a point on the beige carpet. Still she's conscious of his glare and knows without having to look that he's doing that thing where he pulls his chin back so the veins stand up in his neck like thick, tight worms.

That night they have sex for the first time in weeks. She doesn't really want to, but she goes along with it. Anything for an easy life. He is unusually vocal, handling her roughly, and falls asleep straight afterwards while she lies awake in the dark, listening to the muffled sound of a woman crying.

She meets her sister, Nat, in a coffee shop while Charlie is out for the day, getting sponsorship for the site. Nat refuses to come to the flat. 'Ghoulish,' she calls it. Abby says it's fine, but confesses there's an area in the living room where she cannot step, instead sidling around it as if it were a bottomless pit a person could fall into and never come out. Once again, Nat tells her to leave him. 'There are lots of kinds of abuse,' she says. 'Not just physical.' Abby's sister has always overdramatised.

The meeting emboldens Abby.

'You get a kick out of it, don't you?' she says to him over dinner. 'The details of what he did to them.'

'What? Babe, it's just about making money. For you. For us.'

But she's seen the way his fingertips stroke the glossy photographs on the pages of *Francis Downham: Anatomy of a Murderer*, as if feeling for Braille.

After the first night, when she listened to the woman crying, she starts to hear others. Snippets of conversation. Whispers. Sometimes pleas. '*Help me, someone. Anyone.*'

After a while, it does not scare her any more. Instead it helps her feel less lonely.

The site begins to make money. People want photographs. Mementos. One man from America asks for pictures of Abby lying on the bed and in the bath, arranged as the dead women had been. She doesn't want to, of course, but Charlie insists. It's not as if she has to take her clothes off, he says. Now that would be crossing a line.

Still, Charlie isn't as happy as he thought he would be. Since they've been living in the flat, something has crept into his bones and is slowly seeping through the rest of him, like damp. He finds he cannot get warm, no matter what, and there's a spot in the living room that's like a mouth threatening to swallow him whole.

Now it's he who lies awake at night, listening for noises, while Abby sleeps, almost comatose, beside him.

When he does nod off, he dreams of a huge wave rising out of a calm sea, waking just as it smashes on to the shore.

Sometimes he nudges her awake, just to know he's not alone.

He tells her he's been thinking. 'I'm prepared to move. To make you happy.' But she points out how much money they've been making from the site. 'You were right,' she says. He tries to work out why being right should make him feel so afraid. So trapped.

Charlie has always liked them to keep to themselves, separate from other people's interference. 'It's for your own good,' he used to tell Abby. 'You're too soft. People take advantage.'

Now, apart from the Francis Downham groupies, they see no one. Abby no longer wants to leave the flat. Even when he offers to take her out for dinner as a special treat, she refuses. 'We've got everything we need here. It's cosy,' she says. For once there's nothing he can accuse her of, as she's always in his sight. He starts to fantasise about escaping. Getting on a train or a plane. Going as far away from here as possible. But whenever he leaves the flat, he feels he's being followed.

'It's your fault,' he tells Abby, but it's more out of habit than any real anger. Sometimes he feels as if someone has taken a spoon and scooped out his insides so there's nothing there but air.

Charlie is estranged from his family, so no one notices when he stops appearing in public altogether. And he hasn't had a job in years. When the electoral roll form arrives, Abby quietly removes his name from the register. She sells his PlayStation on eBay and spends the money on colour leaflets for the business.

Abby renews the lease on the apartment. The website is doing so well at bringing in an income that the agent doesn't quibble about hers being the only name on the lease. Nor does he ask about Charlie. A single woman tenant is always an easier sell to a landlord.

She makes the place her own. Puts a thick-pile rug in the shape of a heart in the cold spot on the living-room floor so it doesn't feel so desolate. She no longer hears women crying in the soft heart of the night, and it occurs to her that perhaps it was her all along.

Now there's just one human heart on the windowsill, nestling among the cacti so it's scarcely visible. One visitor noticed it and declared it 'almost lifelike' before listing all the ways in which it, in fact, differs from the real thing. People like to consider themselves experts in human brutality, Abby has noticed, just as they might be experts in fossils or fourteenth-century German history.

Nat visits occasionally now that Charlie is no longer here. She has come to terms with the history of the place. Has even come to respect Abby's dedication to what she does. 'You're a bit like a curator, aren't you?' she says.

Abby likes the sound of that. Curator.

Maybe she'll get business cards made.

SCHIAPARELLI PINK BIKINI

MELANIE MCGRATH

Alison slid the bolt and cracked the door, hoping to find Steven on the other side, and was surprised instead to see an old woman, tiny and as wind-gnarled as a clifftop thorn, tricked out in a sparkly sundress and luxuriant wig.

Alison rearranged her face into a mask of friendliness.

The woman's name was Margery. She lived next door. Her rheumy eyes fell on the knife in Alison's hand. Sharp as a tack, evidently.

'Thought I'd come and be neighbourly,' Margery said.

My arse, thought Alison. *The old bat wants something.* Searching for an excuse not to prolong the encounter, she alighted on one that also explained away the knife. Pleased with her ingenuity, she said, 'A bit busy, middle of cooking.'

This was only half a lie. She'd been reviewing tape twelve when the doorbell rang. It was now stopped at two hours twenty-three minutes. At two hours twenty-four minutes the pantie-bitch would appear in frame. At two hours twenty-six a pair of red lace panties (oh, the cliché!) would fly across the screen, and Steven... well, somehow it was easier to watch than to put into words. Over the last few months of her obsession with the tapes, this scene more than any other held her fast in its grip.

A worn gold espadrille slid across the threshold.

'This'll only take a jiffy,' Margery said. She was on her way to a date she'd prearranged on a silver-surfer dating site two weeks before. Her profile had her down as a fit seventy-two and she preferred to meet her dates without her walking stick. Her usual taxi driver had let her down. Would Alison give her a lift to the pier?

'Only I've noticed you park your car directly in front of my cottage.'

The implication was obvious. Margery felt inconvenienced and intended to extract some payback. It was easier, in the end, just to say yes.

During the five-minute drive along the seafront, Margery spoke non-stop, firing off dozens of questions interspersed with tips about the beach and the pier and which fish-and-chip shop served the best battered cod. Where was Alison from? What was she doing in town? Was she going to be staying? To the questions, Alison gave perfunctory replies. To the tips, she closed her ears, preferring instead to think about the knife and what she might have done with it if Steven really had shown up at her door.

As Margery eased herself from the car, Alison leaned over and said, 'So how old *are* you?'

'Eighty-three.' Margery winked. Long false eyelashes fluttered. 'All's fair in love and war, don't you think, dear?'

Alison did think so. Absolutely.

Later, as she was readying herself for bed, Alison wondered if meeting Margery hadn't been some kind of sign, one of those rare moments when fate reached down and tapped you on the shoulder. Perhaps there was a lesson to be learned in Margery's strategic attitude to romance. There she was, a sagging fright of a woman, frankly, but at eighty-three still lying her way into dates with men. If only Alison had been as pragmatic. Instead of confronting Steven with the damn tapes, she might have taken a leaf from Margery's book and found some way to manipulate him into staying. Margery was right. When it came to navigating the treacherous landscape of love, a moral compass was about as useful as a Girl Scout badge.

The following morning began hot. Alison managed to resist watching the Steven tapes before breakfast and decided to take herself off for a swim and use the time to come up with a plan to get Steven back. Though it was early and the beach was nearly empty, there was Margery sitting on a flamingo-themed towel by the groyne, dressed, or, rather, undressed, in a Schiaparelli pink bikini, sea foam tickling her feet. She waved Alison over and, after a cursory preamble, launched into an excitable recitation about yesterday's date. It had all gone marvellously well. Andrew was a retired ship's captain on a fat pension, only sixty-eight and, better still, widowed. Very eager too.

'Plenty of energy, if you know what I mean,' Margery said, laughing.

The sea was punishingly cold. Alison swam out some distance to where the waves came up short against a small sandbank and trod water for a while. She was a strong swimmer, former winner of freestyle sprints at county level, and this had become her favourite swim. At low tide you could clamber on to the sandbank and sunbathe. At high tide the waves swallowed it so completely it was if nothing had ever been there. As her legs motored through their automatic motions, Alison grew hot with righteous anger. There was something unseemly about the old woman's glee.

Something trashy and unconscionable. It was all so unfair. She hauled her body on to the sandbank and in the bright morning sunshine comforted herself with the thought that Margery's romance wouldn't last. Women Margery's age were only really capable of attracting gold-diggers. The retired sea captain would soon see beyond the pink bikini and outrageous wig and move on.

A week passed and Alison saw no more of Margery, but the following Saturday on her way to the shops, she spotted her neighbour once more, shuffling along the pavement arm in arm with a younger man. Feeling herself growing hot and flustered, Alison did her best to slide along unnoticed, but it was too late: Margery had seen her.

'Oh, Alison, dear, come and meet Andrew,' she said in a tone of undisguised triumph.

All thinning sandy hair and phoney, golf-club manner, the sea captain shook Alison's hand, and with oily concern, he said, 'I do hope sound doesn't carry through our party wall.'

'I'm very quiet,' Alison replied obligingly.

'He wasn't talking about you, dear!' Margery hooted, elbowing Andrew in the ribs.

Over the days that followed, Alison replayed this encounter in her mind with a feeling of spiralling disgust. How dare these two has-beens flaunt their antique lust, their horrible, wrinkly happiness?

Andrew hadn't been joking about the noise, as it turned out, but Alison soon discovered that it was possible to drown out the couple's night-time exertions by drinking a lot and replaying the Steven tapes at full volume. It pained her to think about how she'd begged and wheedled Steven to stay, even after he'd moved in with the pantie-bitch, leaving Alison sitting on a shelf made for one. Over the months her awful, humiliating longing for him hadn't subsided. Now Andrew and Margery were rubbing her nose in it. Someone would have to pay.

But who?

The question lay unresolved when Alison bumped into Margery at the post office a few days later, where the old woman was picking up her pension and Alison was posting Steven a death threat and an envelope of toenail clippings. Neither woman mentioned the noisy lovemaking now occurring nightly, and Alison was keen to get away, but found herself giving in to Margery's insistence that they walk back together and – in Margery's words – have a chat, woman-to-woman, and get to know one another better. Alison had no desire whatsoever to 'get to know' anyone, but there was something bulldozery about Margery that made it impossible to say no. The same technique got her dates with inappropriately younger men, Alison supposed.

As they made their way along the seafront, Margery, who was dressed in pink shorts and an off-the-shoulder peasant blouse several decades too young for her, regaled Alison with tales of her conquests. There had been three (or was it four? Alison blanked the exact number) marriages, followed by six blissful years cruising the world with an insurance investigator who called her *tesora* and bought her Janet Reger lingerie. And now, of course, the pièce de résistance, Andrew.

'And what about the loves in your life, dear?' Margery said as they neared home. Alison, who had only ever managed the single conquest of Steven, felt pressured into a rehashed, somewhat reversed version of the facts about an ex-boyfriend so obsessed that the police had been forced to issue a restraining order. In the end, she said, she'd had to leave her home town to escape him. Which was what had brought her here, to the distant edge of the country.

'How dreadful,' Margery said sympathetically. 'Sounds like you could do with a bit of fun.'

'I'm planning on it,' Alison said.

'Amen to that, dear,' said Margery.

The following day a scribbled note arrived under Alison's door with the address of a dating website called Vintage Valentines and the words 'Have fun!' underneath. Alison threw the note in the bin.

A week later Alison returned from one of her rare trips to the supermarket to find Andrew's car parked in her spot and the man himself hauling suitcases through the open front door into Margery's cottage. Alison wound down the window and called out, but Andrew either didn't hear or – more likely – decided to ignore her. She sat in the car with the engine running in the hope that he'd get the message, until the arrival of another vehicle forced her to back down the road into an empty space around the corner. As if it weren't enough to have to listen to the sounds of geriatric sex, Andrew and Margery were now taking what was rightfully hers. Head zinging, nerves at snapping point, Alison grabbed her shopping and began to stomp up the road. Enough was enough!

Margery was now standing in the front garden in a play-suit with her wig skew-whiff, admiring the view. She waved happily to Alison then, gesturing towards Andrew, said, 'Just look at him with all his muscles!'

At this, Margery's beau stopped what he was doing and assumed an ironic (Alison supposed) Muscle Mary pose.

Barely able to contain her fury, Alison hissed, 'Seeing as your boyfriend is so strong and muscly, he can carry your shopping round the corner. I'm trying to be reasonable here, Margery. Andrew is welcome to use my parking spot to unpack, but after that I'd appreciate it if he'd move,' she said, doing her best to keep her voice light. 'This is *my* space and I've got more shopping to unload.'

The smile left Margery's lips and an unmistakably steely glint came into her eyes. Behind them Andrew continued unpacking as if he hadn't heard.

'I've got a bad leg. So we've applied to have that spot switched to a disabled bay.' Margery's eyebrows rose towards her wig and she crossed her arms. 'They give priority to the elderly, you see. From now on, dear, that space is mine.'

'I don't suppose Andrew knows you've been lying to him about your age,' Alison said, before, directing herself to the figure over by the car, she added, 'She's *eighty-three*, you know.'

Andrew looked up, startled.

'Oh, phooey,' Margery said. 'Who's counting?'

That afternoon Alison had intended to do some baking, partly as a distraction from the Steven tapes, but the butter had barely been rubbed into the flour when some urgent impulse drew her to the wine box she'd bought at the supermarket, and before she knew it, she'd drained half and was in the living room gawping at the footage on her laptop, which was so familiar now it was like watching a favourite movie. Almost. Once the wine box was empty, she amused herself by joining in with the soundtrack, taking alternate parts – pantie-bitch's little sighs and giggles, Steven's declarations of lust (God, you're beeeautiful, etc., the same phrases he'd once used with Alison) – until each of the players had somehow become an element of herself and she felt more in control. About two or three in the morning she crashed, insensate, on the bed and woke the next morning to find the computer screen inexplicably covered in depilating cream.

The Monday following Andrew's arrival in the street, Alison noticed the first of a series of small unsettling changes. Traffic cones appeared in what had been her parking spot. Margery's pink-striped wheelie bin was replaced by one in a dull charcoal grey. The following day she spotted Andrew grubbing up the flowers in the tiny garden and replacing them with what looked like cabbages. When she asked what had happened to Margery's delphiniums, he fetched her an alligator smile and said, 'Never you mind about Margery.'

A couple of weeks went by and Friday came around, Alison's least favourite day; it was on a Friday she'd first downloaded the memory stick from the spy camera she'd installed in the bedroom of the flat she shared with Steven, and discovered what she'd already suspected, that her lover was cheating on her with a woman who wore red underwear. On Fridays, as a kind of act of remembrance, she'd developed the habit of staying in bed and watching the Steven tapes all the way through. Today was no different. Fetching a bottle from the fridge, she clambered back into bed with her laptop and poured herself a little light breakfast wine. The footage had only been playing for twenty-six minutes (the real action didn't kick in till three hours twelve minutes forty-seven seconds) when her viewing was interrupted by banging sounds, which seemed to be coming from next door. She clicked pause and held her breath. Nine seconds later Andrew's and Margery's voices came through the wall, his clanging and strained, the words merging into a rackety roar, hers pleading and only just audible. Another bang followed.

Pulling on her robe and a pair of slippers, Alison went outside, overcome by a spiky outrage whose source she didn't really understand, saw Andrew's car parked in her spot and walked over to Margery's front garden. The door was wide open, so she went up the path and knocked. Getting no response, she went inside and called up the stairs. At that moment a shadow fell on the carpet beside her, and, turning, she saw Andrew.

'What are you doing in our house?' There was a stormy expression on his face.

'It's *Margery*'s house, and the door was open.'

To Alison's alarm, Andrew began to move towards her, his body taut with adrenalin, the fists working in and out. Then all at once the stuffing seemed to go out of him and he leaned towards her and snarled, 'I know your type. Pushy. Now go away and keep your nose out of it.'

Alison thought about Steven, and it occurred to her that there was probably a pantie-bitch in Andrew's life and Margery had just found out about her. Alison felt vaguely vindicated and a little superior. It wasn't just Steven, then. Men in general couldn't keep their things in their trousers. Righteousness poured through her like snowmelt. All along Margery had imagined she was happy, when in fact she'd been just another victim. Now it was up to Alison to save her from this creep and pack him off back to sea where he belonged.

'I'm not leaving till I've spoken with Margery,' she said steadily.

A moment later there came a creak on the stairs and Margery appeared, pressing a hand to her cheek as if to cover up some bruising. Her nails were unpainted now, Alison noticed, the acrylics removed. The wig was off and she was wearing a dreary nylon housecoat. A worried smile appeared on her face.

'I'm calling the police,' Alison said. Her head was full of savey thoughts.

'Don't be silly, dear,' Margery said. She came down the stairs and stood in a patch of sun. She looked very, very old.

'Let's just get out of here, Margery.' Alison reached for her neighbour's arm, and as her hand pillowed around soft skin and wasted muscle, the old woman shrugged her off.

'What nonsense!' The place on Margery's cheek where she'd held her hand was unmarked and the steely look had returned to her eyes. 'Why don't you spend some time on the beach instead of hanging around in that bedroom of yours, watching dirty films and spying on your neighbours? And the *drinking*. I daren't count the bottles in your recycling bin. Have you thought of getting help?'

Alison felt a small surge of outrage. She was supposed to be saving Margery. Her neighbour was supposed to be grateful. Just then she heard a gasp and realised it had come from herself.

She blurted: 'You're a disgusting, dried-up old nymphomaniac!'

The old woman cocked her head and shot her a sorrowful smile.

'I'm sorry, dear, but I'm really going to have to ask you to leave.'

Later that afternoon, when Alison went down to the beach to try to swim away the ugliness this latest encounter had left her with, she saw the couple sitting side by side on the sandy strip near the groyne. Margery's Schiaparelli pink bikini had been replaced by a dowdy black swimsuit, and without the armour of her extravagant wig, her face looked drawn and papery, but there was no shadow of any disagreement. On the contrary, Andrew was enthusiastically applying sun cream to Margery's flappy arms, and the two of them were laughing. For some reason the breezy look on their faces struck Alison as ridiculous and a bit sickening. *You wait, Margery,* Alison thought, picking her way across the pebbles at an angle out of the couple's eyeline, *one day you'll come crawling.* Margery's transformation from free spirit to needy, clingy dowd was happening already, only Margery couldn't see it. When Andrew eventually went off with someone younger and more vibrant, someone more like herself, it would be hard for Alison not to tell Margery, 'I told you so.'

Alison was at the shoreline now, her toes digging into the sand, allowing her gaze to drift along the beach. Margery was on her back with her sun hat over her face, giving every impression of being asleep. Her lover was sitting on his towel, with his arms clasped around his legs. Ha! Since the incident, Alison's rage had transferred from Andrew to her elderly neighbour. Alison had never misrepresented herself to Steven, whereas Margery was quite contentedly living a lie and, even now Alison had exposed it, Andrew had chosen to stay. Whereas Steven had made a terrible mistake in leaving, Andrew was making a terrible mistake in staying. The old woman might have all her working parts now, but that situation was unlikely to last. If Andrew didn't get out soon, he'd find himself saddled with a drooling, mad old millstone. At the next opportunity she would tell him the truth, warn him that Margery wasn't all she seemed, that lying about her age wasn't the half of it. The old woman was fake from top to toe.

Alison was up to her ankles in the sea now, the cool water splashing at her shins. An unwelcome thought burst in on her and wouldn't leave. Who would honestly care if she went under the waves and never came back? Who would *actually* give a stuff? Not her dead father or the mother she hadn't seen in years. Not Margery. Not Andrew. God knew, not the pantie-bitch.

The only soul in this world who would give a damn was Steven.

The sea was at her waist now and sending chilly tentacles up her back. She took a deep, steadying breath and dived forward into the water. For a moment her brain froze, and as she rose through the waves, her first thought when it came back to life was that it would be worthwhile dying just to see the look on Steven's face when they told him she was dead. But there lay the irony. She would miss the grand finale. And that made it seem less appealing. She could leave a letter, in which she put the blame for her death firmly on pantie-bitch for stealing her man, or on Margery for rubbing her nose in it and letting Andrew take her parking spot, but the same timing problem applied. There would be a tiny moment of satisfaction, a brief second or two of glee as she contemplated the life-sucking infection of guilt such a letter would spread, but since she had no confidence in an afterlife, all the fun would be in the anticipation.

She took a breath and went under again, surfacing beyond the breakers. The currents in this part of east Kent were unpredictable, and the prevailing westerlies could sometimes push weak swimmers further out to sea. Alison splashed about in the water and came to float on her back on the swell. Above her she could see jet trails and imagine planes packed with luckier, happier people. What if Steven was up there now with pantie-bitch? He'd always been nagging her to go on a mini-break to Copenhagen or Madrid.

She allowed herself to drop back to vertical and began to tread water. The faint outline of the Cap Gris Nez was visible on the horizon. It seemed so close, no more than an hour or two's swim, though she knew that this was just a trick of the light. If she started off now, she'd barely make it as far as the Goodwin Sands. And why would she want to anyway? The only voyage she'd ever longed to complete was the one she had begun with Steven.

Something moved in her peripheral vision, then was obscured by the swell. At first she thought it had to be a seagull, but when the wave passed, she steadied her gaze and saw it was actually a human head. Andrew's head. An arm came up and began waving. Evidently he'd seen her too. He was still some distance from her, but from the manner of the waving, she guessed he was in trouble, asking for help. She stopped swimming and trod water again. The beach was tiny now, the people on it mere specks. Andrew's arm would never be seen in the swell, his voice would never be heard over the relentless whoosh of wind and wave. His mouth was opening and shutting now and she could hear the high-pitched sounds he was making without being able to distinguish the words. As she approached, the waving grew more frantic. Eventually she was near enough to hear him shout, 'What are you waiting for? Help me!'

Alison moved a little closer, but not so close that he would be able to reach her. She wasn't going to risk getting pulled down by anyone, least of all someone who'd got in her face and called her pushy and taken her parking space.

There was a look of barely contained panic on his face. 'I've got a cramp in my right calf and my arm. Can't make the bloody things move. For Christ's sake, help me get back to shore.'

'Only if you stop using my parking space.'

She watched his face fold up in pain.

'You need to promise.'

He made a grunting sound, which Alison interpreted as agreement. She paused before starting again. 'And you have to give up Margery.'

'What?' His face spasmed in pain, but he managed a panicky-looking nod.

Alison looked up at the sky for a moment. The sun was shining and the sky was blue and free of jet trails, and for the first time in a long, long while she felt a burst of happiness. And then it was broken by an almost inhuman groaning sound, which she recognised an instant later as coming from Andrew.

Alison thought about what a heroine she'd be, helping Andrew to the shore. There might be men on the beach who would notice her. On the other hand, it was a long way and at any moment Andrew might start to panic and become ungovernable. Worst case, he might drag them both under.

'We won't make it to the shore together,' she said. 'I'll get you to the sandbank, then go for help.'

A cry of despair escaped Andrew's lips. Evidently this was not the answer he wanted, but sensing he had no choice, he closed his eyes and slowly nodded his agreement to the plan.

Alison swam over and flipped on to her back, curling her arm gently under Andrew's armpit to tow him along. He was stiff with terror and she could feel his heart flapping wildly inside its box.

'Relax, you're making it more difficult,' she said. Tiny bleats still escaped from his mouth, but the softening of his body made the job of pulling him easier. The sandbank wasn't far. Within five minutes they were already approaching its exposed margin. She'd seen its full extent at low tide, but now the area of exposed sand wasn't much larger than Andrew himself. In another fifteen minutes it would disappear under the water entirely. She helped him crawl on to it, his cramped arm useless at his side. His breathing was shallow and he was shivering now.

'Please get help.'

She nodded, but had only gone a few strokes when she felt an impulse to turn her head towards him. And then whatever passed in her for conscience floated off into the water and she spun around and began to plough through the waves once more, slowing down and allowing the currents to take her off course. At this rate it might take her thirty or even forty minutes to reach the shore. She swam on, turning once to check that the sandbank – and Andrew – were no long visible in the swell, then front-crawled until she felt the pull of the westerly current and gave herself up to its drift, enjoying the feeling of being carried ever further from the spot on the beach where Margery was snoozing peacefully on her towel.

THE EDGE

COLETTE MCBETH

E ven after everything that has happened, no one's going to tell me it wasn't real. My friends have given it their best shot. 'Never had you down for a mug,' Dylan said. My mum reckons I'm soft in the head. 'Can't you see it for what it was?'

I tell them I can see it. High definition. Ten million pixels. It's there, burnt into my brain. An image that will never fade.

Half an hour. The time frame blows my mind. It's only because I've read the police reports that I believe it. All those years I've frittered away without so much as feeling a fart pass through my colon, and here I had thirty minutes of life so condensed I could taste its richness on my lips, licked it, felt it pulse through me.

She was sitting under a star. I know what you're thinking. Shoreditch isn't fucking Bethlehem. Stars don't happen, they're burnt off by sprays of halogen from cafés, office blocks, and massage parlours. I hear you. But it was there, a fat gold star that licked yellow light on to her back. She was wearing a dress, bare shoulders crowned by two perfect bony nubs. A small tattoo of a bird sat at the top of one arm.

I would have lingered, drunk it all in, were it not for her position on the roof. Her feet were over the edge, kicking into the night. One hand to steady her on the ledge, the other holding a cigarette to her lips. Her eyes cast downward, as if she were contemplating a sitting dive into a pool. Seven storeys up. A long way down.

It cost me a moment to grasp the situation. *Not her, not that girl who beat out life like a fire.*

'Don't!' I shouted. My intervention was not particularly creative or intelligent. The smallest of frights could have produced the smallest of movements, the kind that would send her hurtling into the night.

She held tight.

I regretted the tone too. From what I'd seen below, she'd had enough of being told what to do.

I pinned her down with my eyes. *Don't move, don't move.* Walked the eight steps across the flat roof to reach her. Each one burnt through my new trainers.

As I approached, she flicked the end of her cigarette upward. The orange dot danced in the dark before it dropped away.

'Hi,' she said, without turning round. 'Have you come to save me?'

My eyes had found her downstairs in the heart of the party. Me, clutching a vodka cocktail, ninety-eight per cent crushed ice, freezing my nuts off. It was summer, but the air-con was winning. I struggled to remember why I was there, when I'd become the guy who ordered a vodka cocktail with elderflower and thought, *Ahh, that's hit the spot.* It was someone's birthday, though whose I couldn't say. A friend of a friend of a friend, me orbiting on the outer reaches of the circle. Laurence, the mate who had persuaded me to come, hadn't turned up. Sent a text by way of apology: *delayed at work*. I cast around for someone to hook on to. All blond hair and icy eyes and teeth so bright they made me squint. That was when I found her.

A piece of real life cut out of the cardboard.

She was standing about five people away. But even from there I could detect the heat. My instinct was to reach out and touch her hair (loose like she'd just rolled out of bed). I'm not a hair toucher by nature and I don't consider myself weird, I'm just being honest about my instincts here. I refrained and inched towards her instead, pressing the crowd away. *'Watch where you're going, man. You spilt my drink.'* When I got close to her, I saw she was attached to a bloke, his arm around her waist, pulling her in too close. His face wasn't all that. She didn't look too pleased with it either.

I watched his lips. 'I saw you looking at him,' he said.

She tried to pull back, but he didn't let her go. She turned her head away from him instead. He put his hand on her chin, moving it back to face him.

'Always the same, aren't you?' He waited for a reaction, the smile spreading up to his black eyes. There was a weariness painted on her face. Like this was an old and tired routine. Like she'd given up trying to breach the distance between his version of her and her own.

'Slut.' A spark in those black eyes. He was finding himself, drawing the power back to his side.

She pushed him away with more force this time. He stumbled back, dazed, stretched his mouth into a smile, made light of it. 'Crazy bitch.'

I saw her weave away from him across the room, disappearing through a door. I was ready to follow in her trail. Only a hand slapping my back stopped me.

'Seb, man, how you doing?'

Billy.

'How's the yoga?'

Yoga. Jesus.

'Hey, Seb, I didn't know you left to be a yoga teacher.' It was Cara, the intern from my office. My old office. 'Oh my God, like, how cool is that.'

'It's early days,' I said.

'Buy him a few drinks and he might show you some poses.' Billy laughed, fat face straining his beard.

It was a week since Billy had called me into his corner of the office – too democratic to have an office of his own – and said, 'I guess you know it's not working out. I mean, creatively – we're moving at different speeds.'

I hated Billy, hated the way he sucked all the good ideas out of me and claimed them for himself. Hated his quiff and his brogues. His offensive nose hair. But this conversation was costing me forty-five grand a year. I had just paid the deposit on a new flat. Billy had waited until it hurt most.

Bastard.

'I didn't sleep with her,' I said. Two weeks ago Billy's girlfriend had tried to pull me at a leaving do. All tears and hands that I'd been forced to unpick from my body.

'No shit.' Billy laughed. 'Like she would.' He shook his head as if the idea was too left-field to consider. 'I'll give you a reference. What do you fancy doing?'

'Me?' I said, because there was no way I was going to beg. 'I've always fancied learning yoga in India.'

'Wow, good for you, man.'

I assessed him. Was he taking the piss? Anyone in the world except Billy would have sensed the remark was soaked in sarcasm. But Billy didn't do nuances. Didn't do depth.

Liked to keep his interactions smooth and close to the surface because there was nothing underneath.

So here I was, rebranded. Seb Cohen, yoga teacher in training.

Billy faded into the crowd, but Cara was warming to the theme. 'I think you're so brave, you know, like I would so love to open up a retreat on Lefkas ... that's so my favourite island of all them. It would have a vegan restaurant too.'

'I thought you liked bacon butties?'

'Sort of ... I mean, not totally. I make exceptions for hangovers. You know, you have to be kind to yourself and just do what you can.'

'I have a question for you, Cara.'

'Go on.' She did this fluttering thing with her lashes that was supposed to be sexy.

'If we all pretend for so long that we forget we're pretending, does that make it real?'

Cara squinted as if the question had got caught up and twisted in the cogs of her mind and she couldn't for the life of her work out how to untangle it.

'I thought so,' I said, and headed for the door that the girl had disappeared through.

'What's your name?' I said. I crouched down beside her, choosing not to look at the toy street and toy people and cars below. The chicken shops, tea parlours with fifty types of leaves, the Thai massage woman that gave extras for a tenner (so I'd heard).

'Belle.'

That wasn't her name. Even then I knew it. When I tell people, they think I'm a moron, but I don't see it like that.

It was a kindness. She was giving me a name to attach my memories to later and keep them clean.

'I'm Seb.'

'Hi, Seb.'

I lit a cigarette and then another. Handed one to her and sat beside her. My legs next to hers.

'I've given up,' I said.

'Me too.' And she took it from me and sucked, and the orange glowed and crackled through the dark.

'Do you think it would be like flying?' She dipped her head down again. My hand reached out to steady her as a siren chased through the streets.

Her face was scratched, a teardrop of blood running down her cheek.

'Your boyfriend is a dick.'

'Was. He's not my boyfriend any more.'

'He didn't look like he wanted to let go.'

'Have you ever tried to make yourself fit, Seb, be who people want you to be? Only to find you can never be the right shape?'

'I'm a rhombus and the whole world is a circle,' I said.

'Yes. That. Exactly. Why do we have to fit? There are so many fucking rules. Tonight I just wanted to do what I wanted to do.'

'And have you?'

'I'm getting there.'

'It takes guts.'

She closed her eyes and inhaled the night like it was the first breath she had taken in a long time. With the cigarette in her mouth, she leaned backwards and raised her arms above her head, every part of her body finding new space, unfurling.

On the inside of each arm, a thumbprint bruise.

'Tell me about yourself, Seb.'

'I was sacked last week. My old boss thinks I'm going to be a yoga teacher.'

'Good choice of job.'

'You think?'

'I do.'

'Your turn.'

'I'm a singer. I'm going to be discovered next week. They'll give me big hair and good clothes, and when it's all too much, I'll find you in an ashram and you can save me again.'

'Again?'

'You're about to save me now.'

She moved away from the edge and asked me to kiss her. With one hand she raised her dress. The world around us was pushed aside to make space for our own, which was the right shape, the right size. Rules swept away.

We dissolved into each other. I didn't know she was carving out an alternative version of that night. Protecting herself against what was to come. Even now I do, I don't blame her.

She gave me half an hour of perfection.

No one can tell me that was fake.

We lay together, watching the planes flickering on their paths, stacking up in the sky. Lives looking down on us. Each a world of its own.

Belle kissed me on the neck. One and then another and another. Three kisses.

'I have to go,' she said.

She walked over to the edge. Sirens bled into the air.

My hand on her shoulder, I pulled her back.

'Don't. Please.'

Tears glazed her eyes.

I flicked my gaze down to see what she was looking at. Flashing lights strobed the dark. Sirens stuttered to a halt beneath us.

'I thought he was perfect, at first,' she said. 'His name was Stephen. He would never have let go.'

A crack had opened up in the sky, sucking our world away.

Her name was Lisa Carey. She worked in a clothes boutique in Shoreditch. She had been with Stephen James for three years. The perfect couple, everyone thought.

'He would have done anything for that girl,' his mother told the *Sun*.

Lisa Carey said they had an argument and he fell. The police wanted to know why she didn't call them, why she didn't run down for help. What happened in the missing half an hour? Why no tears of sadness? They charged her with murder, said she lured him out on to the roof and pushed him.

I'm a witness at her trial. There was an argument, I'll say. He called her a slut. She escaped to the roof. I went up for a cigarette and saw him hitting her, scratching her face. It was an accident, I'll tell them. When she saw what had happened, she was about to jump herself, that's why she didn't race down to see him or call the police. It was me who talked her down.

I saved her.

Now I'm going to save her again.

When I do, she'll come back to me, and I'll never let her go.

THE RAT TRAP

JANE CASEY

The estate agent was a man. Charlotte shouldn't really have assumed it would be a woman. Nikki would be coming to value the flat at five, they had said on the phone, and here was Nicky instead, standing on the doorstep in a tight dark suit that managed to suggest his body was stuffed, like an old-fashioned doll. His hands and face were pale too, like china.

'Is it all right to come in? They did tell you I was coming, didn't they?' He was polite, but there was an undertone of irritation: Charlotte flinched and stood back, mumbling something about losing track of time. She hadn't, of course. She'd been watching the clock all day while she tried to clear out the flat. It was surprising how hard it was to make decisions about the detritus of her parents' lives. Three bin bags were all she had to show for hours of sorting, folding, setting aside.

'I'll try not to take too long. Don't want to get in your way.'

'It's fine.'

They were stepping around each other awkwardly in the small space at the bottom of the stairs. There was more room than usual since the police had taken the coats that had hung on the hooks there – her father's raincoat, stiff with dirt, and her mother's good tweed. Charlotte could still smell the sourness of his body and a faint memory of her perfume. Overlaying everything was the taint of bleach – but that was from the carpet and the walls, Charlotte reminded herself.

'Mind if I go up first?' he asked.

'No, of course not.'

He took the steps two at a time. She followed and found him turning right at the top of the stairs, as if he'd been there before. In a way he had. The maisonettes on that particular road were all the same, built in 1900 to a strict template. Every upstairs one had a narrow staircase that led to a long dark hallway. A sitting room at the front with a box room beside it. Bedroom one. Bathroom. Bedroom two. Kitchen. Steep stairs down to the tiny garden. You could pack a lot of families into maisonettes like that, upstairs and downstairs, both sides of a long road. And now the low-income families were moving out as the prices spiralled higher and higher. Gentrification, the estate agents called it.

'It's very old-fashioned,' Charlotte said, seeing the living room through a stranger's eyes. She was ashamed of the worn fabric on the armchairs, the vile rug on the floor. Above the fireplace there was a lurid painting of Paris, a city no one in the family had ever visited.

'Bay window. Alcoves by the fireplace. Is that a working fireplace? No? Never mind.' He was taking quick measurements, making notes on his clipboard. 'Best thing you can do is clear out all the junk. Old photos, cushions, ornaments, even some of this furniture – get rid of it. These rooms are a decent size, so you want the buyers to appreciate the extra space on offer.'

'These flats always seem to sell quickly.'

'They're in demand.' He gave an elaborate one-shoul-dered shrug. 'Flip side of that is there are lots of them on the market every year. The best ones go fast. Ones like this are a complete renovation job, but you get the developers who are looking for that kind of thing. No one's going to want to live in it as it is, are they?'

Charlotte agreed meekly. She certainly didn't.

It cost her a lot to let the estate agent into her bedroom, the box room. She stood outside, chewing her lip, as he moved around behind the closed door.

'It's good you've presented this as a bedroom,' he called. 'Shows how much you can fit in such a small space.'

Forty-two years of a life, Charlotte didn't say. No one would guess. It was as bare as a postulant's cell, the single bed made up with sheets and blankets and one thin, limp pillow. It was something of an achievement to make a room that was so small look so very bare, but she had few possessions of her own. She borrowed books from the library and kept her clothes in the tiny chest of drawers under the window or on the hooks behind the door. After her mother died, she had worn her clothes too: the same tent-like tunics, slacks with elastic gathers at the waist, shapeless dresses. They had been very alike physically: a scant two inches over five feet tall, with small hands and feet and narrow shoulders that didn't balance out wide hips. They both had long fair hair, thin and almost colourless, along with a pale complexion and watery blue eyes. From behind, her father always said, they were like twins.

Charlotte leaned against the wall, suddenly weak. Sweat prickled under her arms and down her back. She couldn't be sick again. Not now.

'Right, next bedroom.' Nicky almost collided with her as he strode into the hall. 'Sorry! Are you all right?'

'Yes, of course.'

'I didn't see you there.' He flicked the nearest light switch and nothing happened.

'There's no bulb,' Charlotte managed to say. 'It burned out and I haven't replaced it.'

'We should sort that out before viewings.'

Charlotte nodded. *We* meant *you*. She struck off blindly away from him, cannoning off the walls of the dim hallway on her way to the kitchen.

The room smelled stale. She opened the window as wide as it would go and started to wipe down the counters, smoothing away imaginary crumbs and smudges. She hadn't cooked anything for ten days. It was strange how little she wanted to eat now that she was alone.

'Can I just ask – excuse me …'

'Yes?' She skewered a smile to her face as the estate agent leaned into the kitchen.

'Were you planning to clear out the first bedroom?'

'Yes.'

'Because the clothes and everything are really letting the place down. The empty bottles and so forth.'

'Yes.'

'So – just checking – it will be empty when we're showing the place.'

'I said yes,' Charlotte snapped, with no idea how she was going to bring herself to go in there. Then again, it wouldn't be the most difficult thing she'd done recently.

'Is it – was it your dad's room?'

Charlotte nodded.

'And he's the one who just died.'

'Ten days ago.'

'So do you own the flat, then? Don't you have to wait to go through probate?'

'It's in my name already.' Because she hadn't ever had a job and it was advantageous for tax purposes, according to her father. It had been hers on paper, but not in reality. How could it be hers when she hadn't even been allowed her own front door key?

'Do you want to sit down, Miss Cound?' He was frowning at her, concerned. When he dropped the brisk professionalism, he was very slightly camp. 'Shall I make you some tea?'

'No, I'll do it. I'll make some for you.' That was good. That gave her something to do. People who visited liked to have tea, she'd learned when the first of them had called round after the paramedics: uniformed police officers first, and then the detectives and the forensic people. The mugs had collected on the draining board, hastily rinsed, still streaked with brown drips. She had put on rubber gloves and washed them herself when she felt able to do it, up to her elbows in searing hot water as men moved awkwardly around the narrow hall. They had found it hard to work in such a cramped space. There had been swearing, loud at first and quieter when someone remembered she was there. Most of the time she had sat bolt upright in the armchair, not moving, staring at the blank TV screen while the camera flashes flared up the stairs.

She could hear Nicky moving around, jangling the coat hangers in her mother's wardrobe. Her mother had lived and died there, safe behind her closed door, the television turned up as loud as it would go so she was deaf and blind to everything outside her room. It was tidy, at least. A year since she'd died, and Charlotte had only gone in there to clean or to smuggle out a jumper, a shirt, a pair of slacks. Her father had recognised the scarf unfortunately. He wasn't the sort of man to notice much, but he saw the pattern and he knew where she'd found it.

Charlotte found herself holding her hand to her face, pressing it against the cheek he'd slapped as if it still hurt.

'Where's the boiler?' Nicky was back. She pointed to a cupboard near the back of the kitchen and he peered into it. 'Blimey. Museum piece, that. Is there a water tank in the attic?'

She nodded.

'They're a nightmare. So many people want to convert the lofts, you see, these days. I mean, you can fit another flat up there, basically. But the roof slopes a lot front and back, and that great big metal water tank needs to be taken out. They've got to cut it up first and it's not totally legal to use an oxyacetylene torch in a confined space, but don't say I said so.' He made a note. 'I'm not going to tell the buyers about it if they don't ask.'

'Wait.' Charlotte was struggling to keep up. 'You mean they might go up there?'

'Bound to. The prices these places are going for, you've got to make the most of the space. This is where the upstairs maisonettes really score. Yeah, downstairs you've got a bit more storage space and a bigger garden front and back, but you can't extend much. A developer is going to want to convert the loft, make it the master bedroom with an en suite, get maximum bang for his buck. And being frank, that's the kind of buyer we're targeting. You want a quick sale, and they usually buy for cash.'

'But they can't go up there. I've got things up there.'

Nicky shrugged. 'You'll be moving out, won't you? So take your things with you or leave them. Let the buyer throw everything out if you can't dispose of whatever it is.'

'I...I can't. I can't get up there on my own. I didn't think.' How had she managed to forget? Charlotte pressed her hands to her head, appalled at herself.

'It's hard to keep track of everything, especially when you're recently bereaved.' Tactfully Nicky lifted the whistling kettle off the stove and started looking for mugs. 'Teabags? Oh, in here? And do you have any sugar? I shouldn't, really. We're all supposed to be giving up sugar, aren't we? But what's the point of life if you can't indulge yourself now and then?'

Charlotte sat down at the table as Nicky bustled around the kitchen, rattling the teaspoons in the drawer, slamming the mugs down on the counter with careless force. He slopped a little tea over the side as he set her mug down in front of her, and she took a tissue out of her sleeve to mop it up.

'Sorry.' He sat down opposite her and took a sip, closing his eyes briefly to savour it. 'I needed that. What a day.'

'Are you busy at the moment?'

'Hectic. I mean, I prefer it. Keeps you interested, doesn't it? There's nothing as boring as a day when you've got nothing to do except the routine things you always put off.' He laughed.

Charlotte kept her face completely still. Every day had been like that. Every day had always been like that. She'd done her chores – scouring, rinsing, carpet sweeping because her father disliked the sound of a vacuum cleaner, washing clothes, ironing sheets and tea towels and his shirts, dusting, wiping, bleaching, polishing. It had to be done properly. It had to be done carefully. Everything had to be in its place, and the consequences of making a mistake were unthinkable. Her skin smarted at the memories: a hand on the back of her head, forcing her face into the stinging blue water in the lavatory pan until she thought she might drown.

The rim of the mug tasted bitter on her tongue and she put her tea back down without drinking any.

Nicky was staring around the kitchen, still on the clock even if he was taking a break.

'That's sad.' He wrinkled his nose at the little plant by the sink. 'It's dead.'

It was a small jade plant. Its spindly branches had curved downward, the few remaining leaves dull and unwholesome. Charlotte had got it for nothing from the man who ran the flower stall near the train station.

'It's only half dead.'

'If you say so.'

'You needn't worry about it. I'm taking it with me.'

'Oh, right.' His tone of voice showed exactly what he thought of her: crazy. 'Where are you going?'

'I don't know exactly,' Charlotte said. 'Somewhere different.'

'Well, what are you looking for? More space? A bigger garden? A sea view?'

'A fresh start,' Charlotte said. 'A change.'

His eyebrows peaked. 'You could just go on holiday.'

Charlotte had never been on holiday in her life. 'I've been waiting a long time.' Something made her add, 'I don't know if I'm more scared to go or stay here. I sometimes feel I'm trapped and I'll never get out.'

Quicker than she had expected, he drained the last of his tea. 'I should probably be off.'

'What about the loft?'

'What about it?'

'Don't you want to have a look at it?'

Nicky struggled with himself for a moment – it was just on half past five, after all. Professionalism won out.

'Is the access in the hall?'

'You'll need a ladder. It's on the back stairs.'

It was an old wooden ladder, too heavy for Charlotte to lift by herself. Her mother had always helped her before. Two years since she'd been up there.

Nicky grunted with the effort of heaving it into the kitchen. 'They don't make them like that any more. You need to get yourself an aluminium one. You can carry them in one hand.'

Charlotte nodded, as if getting a new ladder was a priority. 'While you're up there, could you get something down for me? It's a blue suitcase – a small one.'

He wanted to say no, she could tell, but he nodded. 'I'll have a look.'

He couldn't miss it, Charlotte thought. There was nothing else up there but the water tank.

It took a bare minute for Nicky to take his measurements. His feet echoed above Charlotte's head. She stood in the hall, her fingers laced under her chin, imagining him lifting the suitcase.

'Look out below,' he sang out, and the bag slid down the ladder: blue leather-effect plastic, strapped with large chrome buckles. The corners were cracked. It had to be as old as Charlotte herself. She ran forward and caught it before it could hit the ground.

'Careful!'

'I thought it was empty.' He came down the ladder slowly and dusted off his hands with a shudder. 'God, I hate heights. I don't even like going up and down the stairs in these places. Too steep for me.'

'That's how he died, you know.'

'Who? Your dad?' Nicky was still wiping his hands on his suit mindlessly.

'He fell down the stairs.' She looked at the narrow, steep treads, noticing again the large gouge his heel or his knee had made in the plasterwork when he tripped over the board she had wedged across the top step. It had been invisible in the unlit hallway as he shuffled down to lock the front door, his unvarying habit before bed. Impossible for him to get a grip on the highly polished handrail; it was, the detective inspector had remarked, like glass. Impossible for him to save himself, especially when he had, as usual, been drinking.

'Did he break his neck?'

'No,' Charlotte said. 'No, he didn't. He cut his head.'

'And that killed him?'

'It bled a lot. Head wounds do.' The blood had been everywhere – all over the door, the wall, the floor. His arms. The leg he'd broken. The doormat was saturated; Charlotte had thrown it away once the police had finally given her permission to clean up.

Nicky was still looking at her as if he didn't understand. She tried again.

'He couldn't get up. He lay down there and he bled. He was on blood thinners, you see, so the cut didn't clot.' She traced a line across her forehead, all the way through her hair to the back of her head, remembering how it had looked. 'That's how rat poison works too. It thins the rats' blood so even a small injury won't heal. They bleed to death. The man from the council told me that when he came to put down poison.' She misinterpreted Nicky's expression. 'Don't worry – that was a year or so ago and we haven't seen a rat since.'

'God.' His face was ice-white in the gloomy hall. 'A cut. You'd think they could have just sewn him up.'

'It happened late at night. The flat downstairs was empty and I was asleep. I sleep very deeply,' Charlotte lied. 'When I found him, it was hours later. He must have been calling and calling.'

He had called and called. He had sworn, threatened, begged, wept. Apologised. Promised.

Died, in the end.

'It was awkward because he was blocking the door. The police had to break in through the flat next door so the paramedics could get to him. We were trapped in here together as he died, and there was nothing anyone could do to help him.'

Lost in the memory, Charlotte barely noticed Nicky saying goodbye, stumbling down the stairs. The slam of the front door brought her back. She carried the suitcase into her bedroom and began to work the stiff straps through the buckles.

They were all there, wrapped up in squares cut from old sheets. She named them quietly, picking them up one by one and laying them back into the suitcase. Thirty years since the first one; two years since the last. Three boys, four girls. She couldn't resist pulling back the cotton folds of the sheet to look at the beautiful, tiny, wizened faces uncorrupted by decay. Babies didn't decompose, she'd learned, when they died before they'd taken more than a breath or two. They had all withered away, delicate as dead leaves.

The flat sold on the first day of viewings for a little more than the asking price, many times the amount Charlotte's father had paid for it in 1975, and she was suddenly rich as well as free. When the taxi came for her, she was waiting on the doorstep. All she took with her was a blue suitcase and a plant that – just that morning – had produced two tiny new leaves the size of a baby's fingernail.

She didn't look back.

Don't Know Where, Don't Know When

Erin Kelly

The feeling was like a small insect – a caterpillar maybe or a slug – crawling up the back of Rachel's leg.

'Don't move,' said Tess, trailing the paintbrush from Rachel's heel to the inside of her knee. She was painting a fake seam over legs 'stockinged' in gravy browning. In wartime real nylons were scarce, but you had to keep up appearances. Rachel had it down to a fine art now, the light brown blending out her freckles. The English lavender scent she'd spritzed herself in was just about winning the battle with the distinctive beefy aroma of Bisto.

'Do you want me to go right up to your knickers?' asked Tess.

'I don't know. We're only here to sing.'

'We'll be finished by five. There's a big band in the marquee at seven. You can't jitterbug with stockings that stop halfway up your leg.'

'Go on then.' Rachel flipped up her petticoats. She was wearing her favourite stage outfit: a flouncy shirtwaister dress with bluebirds printed all over it.

Strong sun cast milky light through the roof of the tent. Fifty wooden chairs were set out in rows, and bunting swayed gently. 'Five minutes till curtain up,' said Tess, even though there wasn't a curtain. There wasn't even a proper stage, just an upturned crate with a single BBC microphone in the centre. Tess tapped it twice and, instead of counting out her soundcheck, said, 'Do you remember that driver, Owen, from last year?' The question was broadcast through the speakers. Rachel crimsoned. Of course she remembered Owen. He was the car fanatic with the huge dark eyes, the black hair Brylcreemed into a glossy quiff, and the steady girlfriend.

Rachel nodded.

'Well, he's single now,' said Tess meaningfully. The words reverberated across the tent and echoed with feed-back. Anyone standing outside could hear them. Theirs was a small community, and gossip spread fast.

'For God's sake, will you come away from that micro-phone,' snapped Rachel.

'Sorry,' said Tess, jumping down on to the grass. 'You should go and find him though, at the racetrack bar.'

That was easy for Tess to say; she could walk up to any man and start a conversation without blushing to her ears. Owen had been a demon on the racetrack but bashful in person; that was what Rachel had liked about him. The girl-friend was the least of Rachel's obstacles. She knew, from a series of unrequited crushes on sensitive introverts, that it was all but impossible for two shy people to get together.

'I couldn't,' said Rachel.

'I knew you'd say that,' said Tess. 'That's why I circled our performance times on his programme. He's coming to the two o'clock show.'

'Tess!' Rachel was thrilled and appalled in equal measure.

'You'll be brilliant,' said Tess. 'Come on, let's get a photograph.'

She pulled her iPhone from a pocket deep in her voluminous dress and switched the camera to selfie mode. Rachel saw them in the screen: red lips, black eyelashes, hair in its victory roll on its best behaviour for once. If they sounded as good as they looked, today would be great.

'Smile!' said Tess, but they both pouted as the camera clicked.

'You have reached your destination,' said the robot voice of the satnav.

The minibus carrying Adua, Curtis, and nine residents of Cedar Falls Retirement Home rumbled towards the racecourse gates.

'Look at that!' shouted Curtis excitedly. 'They've thought of everything!'

The hedgerows were decked with Union Jack bunting. Military-looking cars were parked on the verges. Young people in sludge-coloured suits milled around, and crackly close harmonies blared through roadside speakers. Adua hadn't been born, let alone living in Britain, during the Second World War, but she'd soon picked up on the British obsession with the period, even if she would never understand it. War was something you fled in terror, not something you recreated for fun. Loud noises still brought it all flooding back; on Bonfire Night she had to hide indoors, like a pet.

Curtis had been on a course (he was always going on courses) and come back with a theory that the way to make the residents (you weren't supposed to call them 'old folks' any more) happy was not to force them to live in a world they found alien and threatening but instead to immerse them in the one they had known in their youth. Hence their presence at Goodwood Revival, a motor-racing meet where the sports cars were vintage, and the guests dressed to match.

'Tonight we're gonna party like it's 1949,' said Curtis, to blank stares from the residents. John and Keith wore collars and ties under wattled necks, their service medals pinned on their blazers. The women Adua called the knitters were all in pastels. Rebellious Joyce, at ninety-seven, was taking a stand in a pink tracksuit and Nike Air Max trainers.

And then there was June.

June was the only woman in Cedar Falls who'd kept her hair long. Snow-white, sparse, it was secured in coils by pins. She was a little bird of a woman, skin and bone under the dun flannel of her utility suit. She was haughtily proud of having kept her figure, and Adua felt that June's ferocious intelligence somehow burned the calories away. She had been an engineer and then a university professor; her former students still came to visit her, although there was no family. June had never married, and Adua, who had a radar for these things, sensed heartbreak.

'Come on, June,' said Adua. 'We can go shopping.'

June looked panicked. 'I haven't brought my ration book,' she said. 'What shall I do?'

It wasn't the first time June had faltered lately, and Adua's heart sank. Just because she'd seen this happen before didn't make it any easier. Obviously it was part of Adua's job to tolerate forgetfulness and frailty, but Cedar Falls didn't want you after that. They sent you somewhere else, twice as expensive and half as nice.

'Come on, June.'

'I'll just make myself nice.'

June produced from her handbag a gold compact, the mirror spotted with age, and drew on a red smile. When she pursed her mouth, the lipstick bleeding into the lines of her skin looked like blood vessels bursting.

June made her way across the green, glad she'd worn her lowest heel. The ground was soft, and a woman with a slower step would have sunk deep into the grass. It was a strange kind of fête, this, with clothing stalls outnumbering cake stands and the word *vintage* emblazoned over everything, although there was nothing old-fashioned about the minks and fine dresses that hung on the rails.

'Afternoon!' said a young girl, who had clearly escaped from some kind of travelling circus. She was beautifully dressed, but her arms were tattooed and she had a ring in her nose, like a pig.

'Good afternoon,' said June uneasily, and quickened her pace to catch up with John and Keith.

'We thought we'd give the old folks the slip,' said Keith conspiratorially. 'Head over to the track, see who's driving what.'

'Now you're talking,' said June, but it was hard to give anyone the slip when John was hindered by a walking stick and that girl Adua had seen them go.

'There's afternoon tea in the refreshments tent at two o'clock,' she called after them. 'Don't make me come looking for you,' but there was a smile in her voice. She was a good girl, Adua, once you got used to the accent.

The roar of engines in the distance told them a race was already in progress, but not all the cars here today were taking part. Military vehicles were laid out as though for inspection, although the only serviceman June could see was picking up a little boy to let him look in through the window of a khaki Tilly truck.

'Look at this,' said Keith. 'A Humber Snipe. Haven't seen one of these in a while. Didn't you drive a Snipe, June?'

The past came racing around a hairpin bend, almost knocking June off her feet. She, who never needed a stick, put a hand on Keith's arm. The Snipe, with its mounted headlamps and thick moustache of a grille, had always reminded her of General Kitchener. She'd been driving one when she had first met Ralph. From the back seat, he'd made eyes at her in the rear-view mirror. On their next journey he'd progressed to the passenger seat, and later they'd returned to the back seat together.

'June?' Keith's face loomed into focus. 'Didn't you drive a Snipe?'

'I did, for my sins.' June didn't need to flip open the bonnet to see the workings as clear as day. 'They were tricky to start on a cold day, you had to pull the choke out for a long time, but they cornered surprisingly well.'

They had made her train as a telephonist, but she had a head for machines, not numbers, and after one too many wrong connections, they'd let her work as a driver for the bomb disposal unit. She'd met Ralph on her first week on the job, driving him to an unexploded bomb in a school playground. She'd watched him defuse it with her heart in her mouth. His hands were steady when he was working, but he shook for hours afterwards; that was why he needed a driver. That night, after the keys were locked away, she'd hotwired the car and they'd driven to the coast with the headlights off and made love in the sand dunes. Some men liked their women stupid, but Ralph had loved her knowledge, said that if he only ever spoke to her for the rest of his life, he'd never be bored.

'There's no one like you,' he'd said. 'You're like a man in a nice wrapper.'

It was tempting fate to plan during the war, but they did it anyway. When they were married, they'd work together.

And then, after the war was over, he'd left her for Pam, the meek little redhead who wouldn't know a carburettor from a dipstick but who could cook and didn't want to work. It had been going on for weeks before he told her there was someone else. 'I'll always love you, June,' Ralph had said, 'But you're not *wife* material. I know that now.'

Pam clearly was wife material, with her shopping basket and her perfect red hair swept to one side, a dusting of freckles, that little nose that wrinkled in pity whenever she saw June. The end of the war had been the end of everything for June. She'd known bliss in wartime, and a roaring anguish since the ceasefire.

Soon after their marriage, Ralph and Pam had moved to the countryside. June always thought she would bump into them again. It was a small world, although sprawling all the time. She'd been on the lookout for over sixty years.

They played to a standing-room-only house. It was their most crowd-pleasing set: Vera Lynn and Andrews Sisters classics. The backing track for once played without a hitch, and singing offered its usual release from shyness.

Mixed audiences didn't always work, but it did today. The old folks waved their plastic Union Jacks, smiling fondly at the preschool girls in Peppa Pig T-shirts who danced in pairs in front of the stage. Only one old lady, with coiled white hair, remained stony-faced throughout; blue eyes that didn't seem to blink. The last song always required an internal gear change, from the upbeat close harmonies of 'Boogie Woogie Bugle Boy' to Rachel's solo 'We'll Meet Again'. She closed her eyes to refocus, and when she opened them, a familiar figure was standing at the back of the tent, wearing some kind of military uniform, not one Rachel could identify.

Owen.

She performed to the inch of canvas over his right shoulder; from there, it would *look* like she was singing to him, but she didn't have to risk eye contact.

The applause afterwards seemed to come from a much larger audience. Rachel and Tess held hands for their bow as the chairs emptied. The old lady with the white hair was the second-to-last guest to leave. Only Owen remained.

'I'll give you some space,' said Tess, slipping through the doorway.

'Rachel?' Owen's shyness was at odds with the authority of his clothes. Her fantasy of him throwing her over his shoulder and carrying her out of the tent fizzled to nothing. 'It's Owen. I don't know if you remember me from last year…'

I've thought about you the whole time. I Google you obsessively. I stalk you on Twitter. You're the most beautiful man I've ever met.

'I think so, yes.'

'You sang beautifully, by the way. That last song… not a dry eye in the house.'

'Thanks so much.' Rachel was suddenly acutely aware that her legs were smeared in Bisto. *Sod authenticity*, she thought. *I should've used normal fake tan that doesn't make me smell like Sunday lunch.*

An awkward silence fell, broken only by the roaring sports cars in the distance.

'Aren't you racing?'

'I'm up later. Those are the really early cars,' said Owen. 'Even I'm not insane enough to get inside one of them.' He cleared his throat, clearly working up his nerve. 'In the spirit of the age, I don't suppose I could buy you a pot of tea and a sticky bun?'

Rachel grabbed the last free table in the tea tent while Owen queued at the counter. A wasp dive-bombed the remains of someone else's scones and jam. Rachel waved it away, nearly hitting the occupant of the next table.

'I'm so sorry,' she said, then realised it was the old lady who'd just watched her perform. She had a slightly confused look, like she wasn't quite sure how she'd got there.

Look at the pair of them, fingers not quite touching across the table, all but holding hands. If they didn't make contact, they could still delude themselves that nothing was going on, although June knew that if she interrupted them, they'd spring apart as guiltily as adulterers between the sheets.

'So I've got a new car since last year,' he said. 'A 1948 Maserati E-Type. Two-seater. Obviously it's not actually mine, although that's the dream. I've been restoring it for a collector. New six-cylinder engine. Checked over the bodywork rivet by rivet and sprayed it by hand. Sorry, I'm going all geeky on you.'

'No, it's great,' Pam simpered. She put on a good show of pretending to be shy, but any woman who could steal someone else's man was capable of simpering for effect. June had never simpered in her life, favouring straight-talking and respect over manufactured wiles. *And look where it's got me,* she suddenly thought. *I'd give anything to have him look at me like that again. I'd bat my eyelashes, I'd giggle, I'd play dumb.* A geyser of hot tears sprang suddenly to her eyes; she held them there with muscles she had trained well over the years. Her blurring vision gave her clarity, and she understood that spinsterhood was a small price for integrity.

'Why don't I take you out for a spin in it later?' said Ralph, his eyes glittering with the daring of it.

'Is that allowed?' said Pam.

'Not strictly,' said Ralph. 'But it's wartime, isn't it? Different rules apply.' He winked at her. *I know that wink,* thought June, and her heart contracted. 'We're racing at two o'clock and then again at four, but the track should be free at three o'clock. There won't be any spectators, just people in the bars, and they'll all be too busy drinking to pay us any attention. Meet me at three. If I'm late for whatever reason, just wait by my car. Don't forget, mine's the 1948 Maserati.'

Pam gave a slow blue-eyed blink. Ralph laughed. 'The cream paintwork with a red stripe along the body.'

Pam's smile was vapid. 'I'll look forward to it.'

The couple parted without a kiss, but they weren't fooling anyone.

A champagne tea had been laid on as part of the entry price. The residents got angry if they had to shell out a penny on these excursions, and why not? It cost more to live at Cedar Falls than anyone Adua knew could earn.

Little sandwiches and pink cakes were piled high on doilies. There were three empty chairs.

'John, Keith, where's June?' said Adua when the old men shuffled in. 'I thought I left her with you.'

'She wandered off,' said John. 'You know what June's like. Can't be tamed.'

Adua gave a last longing look at the fondant fancies, then set off to look for June. In the distance, an old-fashioned engine revved with a machine-gun clatter that made her flinch.

Tess stood on a chair, refixing a length of fallen bunting, while Rachel powdered her nose. She saw the old lady in the mirror, over her shoulder, her face working furiously.

When Rachel turned around, the old lady was close enough to touch.

'Can I hel–' she began, but the woman had other ideas. 'You prissy little slut!' Spittle hung in strands between tea-stained teeth. 'Do you really imagine he respects you? Do you really imagine he finds your conversation anything other than stultifyingly boring?'

Rachel took a step back. Her thigh struck the edge of the makeshift stage. 'I'm so sorry, I think you –'

'The only thing you have to offer, and that's all he's after, and that dries up soon enough. I had him first, you know.'

'What's going on?' called Tess from across the room.

Rachel took the woman's hands in hers and felt the ridges of her thumbnail. 'What's your name, love?' she said, as gently as she could manage. 'Is there someone I can call to help you?'

Tess got down from her chair.

'I am not your love,' said the old lady. A coil of hair broke free from its grip and a long white lock hung down next to her face. 'I should like to scratch your eyes out.'

She missed Rachel's eyes but caught her cheek, a sharp fiery graze of fingernails down one side. Rachel's scream was of surprise as much as pain.

'Get off her, you mad old bitch!' Tess grabbed the woman by the upper arms and sat her firmly down in one of the wooden chairs.

'Don't, Tess,' said Rachel. 'She's clearly not well.' Talking hurt, tugging at the cut in her cheek. She put her hand up to her face and her fingertips came away scarlet. Blood always made her feel dizzy, and she closed her eyes and sat down on the edge of the stage. When she opened them, Tess was there with a folded napkin, patting the wound.

'Let's report her for assault,' said Tess. 'I don't care how old she is, she's dangerous. She could have done you some real damage.'

'We need to find whoever she's with,' said Rachel. She turned around. 'And we'll have to find her first.' The wooden chair was empty. They looked all around the tent, but she was nowhere to be seen.

No one had seen June in the pop-up boutiques, where the cool girls sold old-fashioned clothes for twice the price of something new and comfortable. She wasn't in any of the bars that looked like film sets, where beautiful people in silks and suits drank cocktails that cost more than a family meal. She wasn't in the music tent; there were only two girl singers, the blonde one applying a plaster to the redhead's cheek. And she hadn't wandered back to the coach. That only left the racetrack, which Adua had left till last because she knew June had already been there. She set off across the field.

The track that had previously buzzed with engines was now silent and deserted but for a single young man dressed as a soldier, looking nervously Adua's way, then dismissing her when she wasn't whom he was looking for. Adua was on her way back when she noticed a frail figure circling a huge oak tree.

'June?'

She looked like she'd seen a ghost; no, she looked like she was a ghost. Her hair hung loose in wisps around her face, the patches of scalp that were usually covered glowed pink in the sunshine.

'Let's get you fed,' she said. 'You've got time for tea and sandwiches, and then we'll all get on the coach and go home to Cedar Falls.'

June nodded and let herself be led back with uncharacteristic meekness.

She found Owen and his gleaming car round the back of the enclosure. Tools and chamois leathers littered the car park. 'What happened to your cheek?' Owen's mouth was a circle of concern.

'Oh, it's nothing,' said Rachel. 'Just scratched myself by mistake.' She wanted to shut that story down; she wouldn't let her run-in with a poor old lady spoil the moment.

'Oh, poor you,' said Owen. 'Well, madam, your carriage awaits.' He walked around to the passenger side and opened the door with a flourish.

Tempted as she was to feel the wind in her hair, Rachel tied a headscarf under her chin. She had a feeling that she would need to look her best for Owen long into the night.

He turned the key in the ignition; it clapped like an old-fashioned football rattle. 'Don't worry, she always does that,' he said, pulling out the choke. 'She's a slow starter, but a little beauty once she gets going.'

The track curled in a pretzel shape, with one long straight underneath the main bar. Owen took it slowly on the corners, then stepped on the gas as they hit the clear stretch. The guttural engine drowned out Rachel's involuntary whoop. The scenery sped by, so that by the time Rachel noticed the people in the bar, waving in their white gloves and furs, it was too late to wave back.

'This is amazing!' she said to Owen. 'You're amazing!'

He laughed at her delight, showing even white teeth. 'Let's slow her down,' he said as the bend approached. He put his hand on the gearstick, sliding the car into second, and Rachel saw his right foot shift to the brake.

The minibus rumbled back down the long driveway, away from the racing track.

Many of the residents had already unhooked their hearing aids and didn't hear the bang. June heard it. She felt it, like a bomb going off inside her heart.

The minibus driver hit the brake, jerking a dozing Keith awake.

'What the hell was that?' Curtis looked to Adua, who made the sign of the cross with a shaking hand. Slowly June turned to look back towards the racetrack. A thin black plume of smoke was visible over the top of the hedgerow.

'Oh, Christ,' said Curtis, and then June saw him flinch as a secondary explosion produced a huge blackening fireball that mushroomed in the sky. Adua let out a high, childlike scream and threw herself on to the floor of the aisle, where she lay, body and eyes clenched tight. June suppressed an internal kick of impatience. Making a scene never got anyone anywhere.

June looked down at the hands on her lap, the red crescents of blood under her right-hand fingernails and the smears of brake fluid on her fingertips and in the folds of her knuckles. She'd forgotten how those cables leaked when cut.

Wright's Coal Tar Soap, that was what she needed. Lots of hot water. And a good horsehair scrubbing brush. She'd have the devil of a job getting her hands clean.

EL LLORÓN BORREGO

SARAH HILARY

A sticky September evening gobbles up what little shade lies along the street. Papa was right; London is like flypaper.

Mariana trails up the long drive to the big house, a string shopping bag looped over her wrist. She is not in a hurry to reach the back door and the night's work. Through the thin soles of her sandals, her feet burn with the gravel's roll and spit. The drive is a dry river between lush banks of lawn, where the sprinklers have been switched off for the day, so she cannot even stop and wet her face and hands.

At the back door, she slips off the sandals and pulls on a thick cardigan and thermal gloves, knotting a heavy shawl around her shoulders. She bends to roll wool socks up each leg, ignoring the creep of sweat at her neck. She pulls the empty shopping bag flat and pushes it into the pocket of her dress. In layers enough for winter, she eyes the doorway to the Ice Gallery.

A bird purrs somewhere high behind her. She turns to look at the patchy shade she is leaving. The pale bends in the driveway are like the elbows of the Guadalquivir, where she played with her brother, Toli. She sees again the green light gusting above the swamp, squatting in fists over the muddy skin of the river. They would throw stones and wait to watch the mud make its grab, sucking each stone down before sending up blisters that burst and spattered. She teased Toli with a lie about a dead horse in the swamp or, 'Maybe it's a man. He wandered off the path and drowned, inch by inch.' She jumped at Toli, grabbing his ankles so he squealed and wriggled. 'The cold mud crept up his legs –' she walked her fingers to his shins and pulled with her palms at his knees '– drinking him down like broth –' Toli flung his thin brown arms around her neck and held hard.

Tonight she must scrub the scum that settles, always, on the marble floor of the Ice Gallery. Down on her hands and knees, rubbing, shuffling backwards a foot at a time. Checking across her shoulder as she goes, taking care not to knock into anything. She could not begin to pay if she did.

Her skin shrinks at the thought of the work ahead of her. Some nights she fears her hands will freeze to the floor she is polishing, that she will be found the next morning glued to the marble like a new sculpture, her face frozen in a scream, her tongue furred with frost.

Perhaps then the Ice Gallery's owner would notice her – if she were a part of his art collection rather than merely its caretaker. Bartholomew Rye is a busy man, a connoisseur. He doesn't have time for cleaners, or servants of any kind. He does not even know Mariana's name.

She saw him once. A big man balanced on the balls of his feet like an anxious matador. He wore a purple felt fedora and a red sweater up to his chin, and he had little hands he could not keep still, fussing everywhere, petting his art – his animals – as if it were all still alive. Mariana stayed on her hands and knees, watching him. He had a drink in a slim glass. She heard the squeak of ice, the tinny fizz of bubbles. She thought, *He is a man who knows how to look after himself.*

He has hung a tiger at one end of the Ice Gallery. She imagines him hunting it, though she knows he did not. Bartholomew Rye buys his art from other hunters, other slaughterers. Two men, she imagines, dropping the tiger with its coat still fiery down at his small feet. Alone in the gallery, she will sometimes reach a hand between the big cat's frozen jaws to feel the thin sting of incisors. She is not allowed to touch his art – his animals – so she turns the touch into dusting, plucking imagined cobwebs from the tiger's wide-dead mouth.

'This is Mariana,' they could have said. 'She will clean for you. She is a good girl, strong and careful. She misses her brother, her home. You are lucky to have her.'

And Bartholomew Rye would have said, 'I am lucky to have her.'

Instead, he does not know her name.

One week ago, they gave Mariana a new machine for polishing the floor.

She loves this machine, with its handsome cushion of thick grey felt that glides across the marble at the press of a switch. The polisher cost more than she is paid in a year. She takes it as a sign that she is trusted, for her employer to make a gift of such a machine. Her arms tremble as she winds its long flex at the end of each night, the palms of her hands bright with its buzzing. When she holds her hot fingers to her face, she smells beeswax and lanolin. But the polisher's long flex leaves scuff marks and she is soon down on her knees again, working the cloth with her hands, raising from the marble a shine so lethal she finds her face in it.

Everything in the Ice Gallery, she has been told, is beyond price. Everything. Even the dead sheep with its suckling lamb, beyond price.

The bird purrs, high in its tree.

The gravel in the drive glitters like eyes.

Mariana stands in her many layers, looking out across the lawns to where London climbs with all of its doors and windows, dusty, dim. The armpits of her dress are soaking wet; she must get inside before she melts. She turns and shows her face to the camera mounted over the door, waiting to be let into the building by Gerald, the security guard.

She hopes he is too lazy tonight to come up from his room in the basement. He likes to look at her and sometimes to touch, pretending he is checking that she does not have hidden equipment to photograph the priceless art or to steal it away. He makes believe that Mariana's cardigan has secret pockets. But he cannot bear to be in the Ice Gallery for long, not even to watch her down on her knees. It is far too cold, and he is far too fat. A little man who likes to be comfortable, but Mariana thinks that he could be vicious if she gave him an excuse. So she smiles blandly at the security camera and ignores the stabbing of sweat at the small of her back.

She is thinking of her mother's advice always to pick ugly – of fruit like figs and tangerines. Picking ugly means appreciating everything, giving thanks for everything. Mariana and Toli always chose the ugly oranges with the scarred skin and the juice that filled their mouths with colour, staining Toli's thin brown fingers to pink.

The back door buzzes open.

Mariana makes no noise along the corridor.

A white powder of light shows under the door to the Ice Gallery. She stops, one foot raised, listening with all her ears –

Something is wrong tonight.

From under the lip of the door, no icy teeth come to nip at her toes. No grumbling from the machinery that keeps the temperature far below freezing. Just a soupy silence broken by the sound of something dripping.

Her nostrils flare. There is a burning at the back of her eyes.

Oh, she thinks. *I know this. I know... this.*

A day comes back, when she was six. Dressed for church, her ankle socks spotted, rusty with blood. Mama is cross with her, dapping a wet handkerchief, making it worse.

'No place for girls,' Papa said of the abattoir.

Toli went to work in the abattoir when he was twelve. Mariana was taught to cook the meat and to sluice the deep grooves in the tiled floor, but it was men who hung the cattle, peopling the cool dark place with carcasses that swung their shadows across the ceiling and up the walls. Not a lot of money in dead meat; Mariana was sent here to scrub the floors of men who did not know her name, swaddled in layers she hoped will hide her curves from the fat little guard who coveted her comforts.

I know this, she thinks. And her arms ache for her brother, for the Guadalquivir with its blisters that burst and spatter, and for the story of the dead man that made Toli cling to her.

The Ice Gallery is warm and stinking. The stench is so ripe and round, her stomach makes a fist. It is the smell of her uncle's abattoir, where the slaughtered cattle dripped on to the tiles.

At the threshold to the Ice Gallery, she crosses herself quickly, lifting the hem of her cardigan to cover her nose. Sweat sticks her dress to her breasts. Her lips move in a prayer taught to her by her grandmother: 'Sweet angel. My sweet angel, pray with me. Pray for me in the morning and in the evening always. Don't ever leave me. Don't ever leave me alone.'

In the Ice Gallery –

Plink-plink is the only sound.

From high up, falling.

Plink-plink. Plink.

Mariana opens the door and sets her eyes to the ceiling, knowing what she will see.

The fleshless face of the lemon shark grins back at her, its long jaw slanting forward, carrying countless teeth. But it is not the lemon shark that is dripping. It is not the lemon shark and it is not the tiger with his sharp teeth that prick her fingers.

Gerald is at her elbow, gasping and wobbling with shock.

Mariana steps back when she sees the steady seep of crimson-black. An awful tide that creeps across the marble, towards her socked toes. *Plink-plink-plink.*

She looks for the place where the polisher is kept, its long flex wound away, its plug still socketed to the wall. The other plug, the wrong one, has been pulled free. Everything in the room is ruined. Beyond help, as it is beyond price.

'How...?' Gerald cannot make sense of the mess. 'How –?'

'Didn't you check the room earlier?' Mariana asks.

It is his job to check, but he is lazy and does not like the cold.

Plink-plink-plink. Plink.

And now she hears the high tapping of leather soles down the stairs of the house, across the chequered black-and-white tiles towards the Ice Gallery.

And here is Bartholomew Rye in scarlet pyjamas and a skull-tight tarboosh sewn with sequins, a white handkerchief held to his nose. He does not see Mariana. He only sees the mess.

'What?' he cries. 'What?'

His hands flap. He reaches up and does not look down, and the flex of the plug is a snake under his feet.

Mariana watches him rear away from the marble that is wet now and red, and which she lavished with beeswax and lanolin and the thick grey felt of his expensive gift.

He rears up and he does not come down, not for a long moment.

His feet flap like his hands. He reaches for the lemon shark. He reaches for the sheep, making a noise it might respond to were it alive. Bleating at the ceiling and now –

Down he comes with the terrible crack of his head hitting the floor, spilling its colour and smell, and she watches the grouting fill and thinks of how she will have to get it clean tomorrow. After the police have come.

Gerald is crying in the corner. He does not understand what it means, not yet. No more Ice Gallery. No searching for stolen treasures in the pockets of her cardigan. No Bartholomew Rye. A boat back to the Guadalquivir, to the green light gusting above the swamp and her brother, Toli, and the ugly oranges running their sweet colours into her mouth.

Mariana lifts up her skirts from the spreading red. She smiles at the sheep and its suckling lamb. No longer frozen, it is weeping.

Plink-plink-plink.

Its tears have made a tide across her polished floor that reaches around the shattered head of Bartholomew Rye to her socked toes.

'*Borrego*,' Mariana breathes into the hem of her cardigan. '*El llorón borrego.*'

The weeping lamb.

STOP THE PIGEON

LOUISE VOSS

June 1992

'It's just a *joke*,' was Ashley's common refrain as he stretched cling film over the toilet bowl or put laxatives in Chaz's coffee. 'Some people have no sense of humour.'

He wasn't afraid of making loud personal remarks either. One of his favourite topics was his colleague's slight frame and short stature. It was partly born of jealousy – Chaz, although he was close to (as Ashley was wont to point out) 'nine stone soaking wet', had a leonine mane of hair, whereas Ashley's coarse offering was receding almost too fast for him to keep up with. It was currently pleasing to Ashley to note that Chaz seemed to be getting thinner by the day, and his hair wasn't as good as it used to be either. It had got distinctly brittle-looking and dull.

Ashley was still jealous though.

'See that bag?' he loudly asked Shirley, their shared PA, as Chaz walked into the open-plan office, carrying something in a Tesco's plastic bag. 'It's got a brick in it. It's to weigh him down and stop him floating away.'

'Oh, piss off, you lardy git,' was Chaz's retort as he passed Ashley's desk, but the words lacked sting. Chaz had, Ashley pondered, been a bit quiet in the past couple of weeks.

'Shut it, runt.' Such was the sophisticated ebb and flow of their banter.

Shirley just curled her lip and rolled her eyes when neither of them was looking. She found their whole 'banter' thing unutterably tedious.

Things were currently a bit slow in the Drama Department of London South Television. Neither producer had anything in production, just the usual vague talk of projects 'in development' that never seemed to materialise into anything, but which necessitated regular three-hour lunches with various casting directors, agents and actors.

Chaz was the most recent of the pair to have had anything broadcast – a two-part serial-killer thriller called *The Matchbook Murders*. The first episode had gone out the previous week and, as always, dozens of letters of both praise and complaint had flooded in from viewers with an over-developed sense of outrage and/or too much time on their hands.

The fruity language and verging-on-gratuitous violence of *The Matchbook Murders* had provoked mostly negative feedback from the letter-writing public, but this was no surprise to anyone. Chaz didn't seem to care anyway, and why would he? The ratings were fantastic, much to Ashley's seething envy. His own last production, a lacklustre six-part costume drama nearly a year ago, had been a resounding flop.

Shirley was now typing up the standard reply letter of mollification and apology for offence on her word processor, and Ashley gazed across the room at her profile as she frowned in concentration, her fingers flashing over the keyboard and her eyes glued to the screen.

She was lovely to watch, was Shirley. She had a lithe dancer's body, the neatest nose and perfect, rosebud lips. Everybody fancied her, but she was far too annoyingly dedicated to her job to respond to his or anyone's advances. He permitted himself a small daydream about being sequestered in the stationery cupboard with her and smiled to himself, smugly, as though it was fact and not fantasy.

'What are you smirking at?' Chaz called from his desk, through a mouthful of the cheese-and-pickle sandwich he had removed from the Tesco's bag.

'Just thinking about how the first thing I'm gonna do when I get promoted is fire your skinny arse,' he retorted. It was also annoying to him that Shirley seemed to have an inexplicable fondness for Chaz. What did that runt have that he, Ashley, didn't?

'Fighting talk, big man.'

Ashley could tell that he'd riled his colleague – interesting, he thought. He didn't really think either of them stood a chance of being promoted to the newly vacant position of Head of Drama, although each knew the other had applied and been interviewed for it. It was open to external candidates too, which made it less of a certainty that one of them would get it.

'Make us a coffee, Shirley darling, would you?' Ashley asked abruptly, turning back to his computer screen and the *Secret of Monkey Island*, the game he played almost obsessively when their boss, Brian Innes-Hopkins, was out of the office.

'Sure,' Shirley said, uncurling her long torso from her office chair. 'Want one, Chaz?'

Chaz nodded. 'Thanks, love.' Wiping his mouth with the back of his hand, he got up too. 'I'll give you a hand.' He followed her out as Ashley muttered, 'I bet you will, you dirty bastard.'

When the two had left the room, Chaz hitching his chinos up over his narrow hips, Ashley looked around. He was alone – everyone else was out on their lunch break.

He sprinted over to Chaz's desk, just to have a nose around at the memos he kept impaled on a spike and the latest emails on his computer – what if Chaz had been offered the Head of Drama job, and he, Ashley, just hadn't yet been informed? It would be beyond humiliating.

Thankfully there was nothing on the spike or in Chaz's emails to indicate any such thing, so Ashley sauntered over to Shirley's workstation next, keeping a weather eye on the door.

There was a standard letter on the screen of Shirley's WP, to one of their more regular and vociferous complainants, a Mrs Hetty Stinchcomb of Winterbourne Prior, Wiltshire. She was chairlady of the Wiltshire Ladies' Voluntary Listening and Viewing Association and frequently complained about London South Television's drama offerings. Her objections included but were not limited to sightings of men in their pants; any use of bad language, including the word 'damn'; mumbling actors; overly loud incidental music; and the merest flash of a woman's bosom. You name it, she moaned about it.

Dear Mrs Stinchcomb,

Thank you so much for taking the time to write to us again. I am so sorry that the first episode of The Matchbook Murders *did not meet with your approval. We do welcome our viewers' opinions, good or bad, in an effort to continually improve London South Television's drama output. Of course, our intention was not to shock anyone, but we felt that a certain amount of violence and swearing was appropriate and indeed necessary to the plot, and transmission was post-9 p.m. watershed. Again, I do apologise if it caused you any distress.*

Yours sincerely,

Chaz Gest

Producer

Ashley hesitated just for a second, took hold of the mouse and moved the cursor up to the last sentence, deleting it and bending over the keyboard to replace it with *'And frankly, if you took that poker out of your arse, you shrivel-ovaried old harpy, you might stop whingeing about everything and enjoy life a little more. Do me a favour – piss off and stop bothering us, would you?'*

He chuckled and moved back to his desk, sure that the eagle-eyed Shirley would notice before she printed it off and posted it. In the grand scheme of pranks, it wasn't much, but Chaz's annoyance when he spotted it should be worth a laugh or two.

However, by the time Chaz and Shirley reappeared with three mugs of coffee between them – Ashley sniffed suspiciously at his before taking a sip – the screensaver had kicked in on Shirley's WP and she then got busy sorting through Chaz's expenses. Ashley quickly forgot about his little editorial addendum.

'Soon you'll be wearing my sword like a shish kebab!' he shouted at one of the on-screen pirates on Monkey Island, utterly engrossed in the game.

The rest of the afternoon passed by in a pleasant blur of minimal activity, uninterrupted by any actual work further than flicking through a couple of scripts. It was only when Chaz put on his coat and made a rude hand gesture of farewell in Ashley's direction that the latter recalled his prank and was surprised at the lack of abusive feedback he'd had in return.

'Hey, Shirley,' he said, once Chaz had exited, 'what did old scrotum-face think of our new letter to Wincyette Stinchcomb?'

Shirley cocked her head to one side, her perfect curtain of glossy dark-brown hair swinging in graceful accompaniment. She resembled a Crufts-winning spaniel, Ashley thought. He wished, not for the first time, that he could tell what she was thinking, but her face was always a perfect mask of neutrality.

'What do you mean?'

He sat up a bit straighter. 'The letter. It was on your screen. I changed it a little teeny bit while you were making the coffees earlier.'

Shirley regarded him coolly. 'It's gone. I took all the post down an hour ago.'

'*WHAT*?' Ashley shot out of his seat.

'What's the matter? How did you change it?'

He ignored the questions. 'Didn't Chaz notice it when he signed it?'

Shirley bit her lip. 'I suppose he can't have done.'

'Well, then, how come you didn't, you stupid bitch?' Ashley yelled, the harsh words bubbling out of him like milk boiling over. '*You* printed it out! We have to stop it! You know what Stinchcomb is like – she complains about everything as it is! She'll have our guts for garters. We'll all be fired!'

Shirley gathered up her coat and bag, her lips in a tight line. 'I'll not be spoken to like that, by you or anyone,' she said, switching off her computer and heading for the door. 'You'll have to stop it yourself. I'm going to the loo, and then I'm off home.'

'Don't you dare! If you leave now, that's it, you're the first to go. Goodbye, Shirley; bah-bye; *sayonara*, baby – hello, P45...'

Shirley planted her hands on her hips and narrowed her eyes at him. 'You can't fire me, Ashley. *Brian* is my line manager, not you.'

And she was gone, slamming the door of the ladies' theatrically behind her, the most emotion he'd ever seen her display.

'Shit!' Ashley muttered. 'Shit, shit, shit.' He grabbed his black leather jacket and ran out, thundering down the stairs three at a time, ricocheting around corners and pushing through the revolving main doors so fast that he almost knocked himself out.

He caught up with Chaz in the car park as he was unlocking his red BMW – which, as usual, was parked across two spaces, as though he'd slalomed into it blindfolded that morning.

'Chaz, mate,' he panted, a stitch in his side making him lean heavily on the car's bonnet with both palms. 'I've done something –'

He stopped, managing to straighten up. It was hardly his fault that Shirley was an unobservant bimbo. '*Shirley* has done something really stupid ...'

As he filled Chaz in on the prank, it gave him a small amount of gratification to notice the colour seeming to drain out of Chaz's already pasty face. Then the other man gave a weak bark of laughter and slapped him on the shoulder.

'Nice one, Ashers. Very good – you had me there for a minute. Now piss off – there's a decent bottle of Cab Sauv with my name on at home.'

Ashley groaned. 'No. I'm not joking. We have to get that letter back!'

'You bloody idiot,' said Chaz, slamming his car door closed again. 'What are you waiting for?'

Both men charged across the car park towards the post room situated by the entry barrier, Chaz's messenger bag bumping against his hip as he ran. It was strangely lumpy, making Ashley think once more of his earlier gag about Chaz needing to be weighed down.

The mailroom was empty apart from a Youth Training Scheme trainee with floppy hair and baggy jeans, who was idly stamping 'SECOND CLASS' up his arm as he sat with his feet up on a desk. The Inspiral Carpets' latest song blared out from a transistor radio nearby, and the boy inked his arm in time to the beat.

'Oi, you!' Ashley said. 'Where's today's post?'

The boy gaped and froze mid-stamp. 'Gone,' he said, hastily removing his tatty Nikes from the desk. ''Bout half an hour ago. Keith took it in the van.'

Chaz and Ashley stared at each other. 'Where to?' Chaz demanded.

'Sorting office.'

'Well, obviously,' snapped Ashley, advancing on him. 'Which one?'

He looked terrified. 'I dunno! I'm new, i'n I!'

Ashley continued to advance towards him with such menace that the youth dropped the stamp and backed himself against the wall, his palms flat, turning his head to one side as Ashley loomed into his face, sweating and shouting.

'Now you listen to me, you little scrote, I don't care if this is your first day, but I promise you this: it will be your last *on this planet* unless you find out immediately where Keith has taken that post and get him to bring it back NOW!'

The boy was almost crying as he broke away and ran across to the phone. 'I'll call Bill in Transport,' he stammered. He was shaking so much he could barely hold the receiver. 'Bill? It's Kieron in the post room. I've got, um –'

'Ashley Lynes and Chaz Gest,' said Ashley through gritted teeth.

'– two men here who want to know where the post goes. They says it's urgent like ... Right ... Fanks, geezer.' He hung up. 'West Kensington Depot,' he gibbered. 'Blythe Road.'

Chaz had grabbed an *A to Z* and was already flicking through it. 'Let's go.'

'We'll take my motor,' Ashley said as they pounded back across the car park like a budget *Starsky and Hutch*, Kieron's whimpers still in their ears. 'You navigate.'

The engine of Ashley's silver Jag gave a guttural roar as he floored the pedal and they raced off. The atmosphere inside the car was toxic with stale cigarette smoke and the rank scent of unspoken fear.

'Mate, you've gone too far this time,' Chaz said eventually as they pulled up at a red light.

'Oh, lighten up, cockblanket,' Ashley retorted. 'We'll get it back.'

'We'd better. Brian won't give either of us the promotion if he finds out.'

My promotion, thought Ashley.

But when they got to the sorting office, no amount of *Don't you know who I am*s and toys thrown out of prams would cut the mustard with the implacable red-jacketed post-office employees. Apparently the truck bound for Salisbury – the closest sorting office to the village where the letter was headed – had just departed, with Mrs Hetty Stinchcomb's typed time bomb on board, and there was nothing they could do to stop it.

Ashley looked at Chaz. The man's face seemed to have turned from pasty to greenish grey. He clapped his hands together with a meaty thwack. 'There's nothing for it, my old mucker. Wiltshire, here we come.'

'You aren't serious.'

'Deadly, my little friend, deadly. Road trip! If we leave now, we might get to the Salisbury sorting office before it closes – or bribe one of these fine gentlemen's southern colleagues on a night shift to let us in' – here he gestured to the gaping postmen – 'and if all that fails, we wait outside

Stinchcomb's gaff and intercept her local postie on his morning rounds. Easy!'

Chaz opened and closed his mouth – speechless for once, Ashley noted. He could almost see Chaz's mind whirring through the alternatives and finding them wanting.

An hour later the two men were stuck in a five-mile tailback on the M3, both of them smoking furiously. When they stopped at Fleet Services for Ashley to have a rest stop – he had a very weak bladder – Chaz announced that he'd stay in the car and ring Shirley to sweet-talk her into returning to the office to get Hetty Stinchcomb's address (neither of them being able to remember it with any more specificity than the name of the village).

Ashley dashed in, peed, purchased fags and dashed out again, ripping the cellophane off the fresh pack of cigarettes as he hurried back to the car. Then he stopped short, staring.

Chaz was in the car, speaking on Ashley's brick-like car telephone, but rather than the facial expressions that Ashley assumed would accompany Chaz's bribes of year-end bonuses and slap-up lunches in restaurants of Shirley's choosing, the man looked as if he'd just been told his dog had been run over. Were those *tears* in his eyes?

Chaz spotted him approaching and seemed to rearrange his features. By the time Ashley was sinking his bulk back into the driver's seat, Chaz was scribbling Hetty's address on the inside of the recently finished pack of Marlboro Lights, still on the phone. Ashley could no longer read his expression.

'Thanks, darling – can't believe you remembered it off by heart. You're a star.'

Ashley snorted. They wouldn't be in this mess in the first place if the stupid bint had done her job properly.

Chaz turned away and looked out of the passenger window, covering his mouth with his hand so that Ashley had to listen hard to hear what he said to Shirley next.

'I mean it, you're a doll. Don't let anyone push you around, ever. You're a top secretary. And – I just want to say – thanks, like. Thanks. For everything.'

He hung up the phone and stared straight ahead, a muscle ticking in his jaw.

Ashley frowned. 'What the fuck was that all about?'

Chaz didn't speak.

'Chaz? What's the matter?'

Eventually Chaz shrugged. 'Just feeling philosophical, big man. Not something you'd know much about.'

The traffic began to move again, picking up speed. Ashley overtook a woman in a Capri, earning himself a dirty look from her.

'Seriously though – are you OK?'

'I'm fine,' Chaz said. 'Let's play I-Spy. I spy with my little eye something beginning with F-E.'

'Fuckin' eejit,' Ashley replied without hesitation. 'And I suppose you think that would be me, but I would say take a long hard look in a mirror. I mean, who signs letters without checking them first?'

Normality restored, the rest of the journey to Salisbury proceeded without incident. With the aid of the *A to Z* and the assistance of several helpful pedestrians, Ashley and Chaz reached the sorting office by 7 p.m., hungry, irritable and, in Ashley's case, in urgent need of alcohol.

'Oh no, sir,' said an unctuous fat controller-type when they had explained their plight. 'I'm sorry, but we can't intercept a letter once it's here. They don't get sorted till the early hours, ready to go out for delivery at 5 a.m. And even if I could lay my hands on it at this moment, I'm afraid it's against the law for me to give it to you unless you can show me proof that one of you gentleman is the addressee ...'

'Fuck's sake,' Ashley said, rage percolating. 'Why are you people all such jobsworths?' His shirt was sticking to his back, his arse ached from sitting in the car for so long, and his fist was twitching to punch the post-office employee.

'Come on, Ash.' Chaz put a hand on his arm. 'It was worth a try. Let's go and have a pie and a pint.'

As he escorted his colleague away, Chaz added, 'Plan C it is, then. We'll just go to Winterbourne Prior and wait for the postie outside Stinchcomb's house in the morning. It's not the end of the world.'

Winterbourne Prior turned out to be little more than a hamlet with a church and – much to Ashley's huge relief – a village pub. Once they'd scoped out Widow Stinchcomb's gaff (Ashley insisted on calling her that, although, of course, he had no idea of her actual marital status), they repaired to the hostelry and settled in for the evening.

'Well,' Ashley said, sinking back into a high-backed uncomfortable wooden bench, his first pint half gone in seconds.

'Well,' Chaz echoed. They regarded each other with something that Ashley thought might almost approach affection.

'Cheers, twat.'

Ashley raised his glass and Chaz chinked it with his own.

'You got an alarm on that thing?' he asked, gesturing towards Ashley's expensive Rolex. 'Set it now so we don't forget. Five a.m. should do it; we don't want to miss the postman.'

Ashley obeyed, already struggling to clearly see the dial on his watch as his fat fingers fiddled with the little wheel.

That done, he felt as if he could stop worrying for a few hours.

The table between them became increasingly sticky with spilled beers and cluttered with uncollected empties, too many to count – if Ashley had been sober enough to do so.

'You're not bad, really, for a bastard,' he slurred, six pints in. 'I'm sorry, like, for being an asshole.'

'You are a proper asshole too.'

'You're not supposed to agree with me! What are you, my ex-wife?'

'No, thank God. It's bad enough being your colleague.'

'You love me really though, don't cha?'

'No. I hate you.' Chaz's face was too straight for Ashley to know if he was joking or not.

Ashley planted his elbows on the table. 'Changing the subject...' he slurred, 'that promotion. You definitely had an interview for it, or were you winding me up?'

'Yeah, I did. Did you?'

'You know I did.'

Chaz swirled the dregs of his Coke around the glass.

When had he switched to soft drinks? Ashley wondered.

'How many of us on the shortlist?' he asked, trying to sound as if he didn't much care.

Chaz shrugged. 'Don't know. A few, I think. We'll find out in the next couple of days.'

'That's what Brian told me too. But mate – hands off. I mean it. That's *my* fuckin' job.'

Chaz laughed mirthlessly. 'Who knows what's going to happen? We'll just have to wait and see.' He stood up. 'My round, I think. Let's not worry about it tonight. If we don't get that letter back, Brian will fire both our arses anyway, so' – he spread his arms wide and threw back his head – 'let us drink, drink and be merry, for tomorrow we may dieeeee.'

'You poofter,' Ashley grunted. 'You're on the frigging Coca-Cola! Get us some pork scratchings while you're up there, would you?'

Chaz bowed exaggeratedly. 'Your wish is my command, oh plump one.'

Ashley squinted after him. The man was so weird, he thought. Manic one minute, all quiet and depressed the next. He wasn't drunk, so why was he acting like that? And what was all that about with Shirley on the phone earlier? Chaz was usually so … boring.

Still, he pontificated drunkenly, he hardly knew him at all outside of the office. He'd never even met his wife.

'How's the wife, Gest?' he asked when Chaz returned with two fresh drinks.

Chaz's already narrow eyes seemed to squinch together even more. 'Fine. Playing a lot of squash at the moment.'

'Oh, right.' The comment somehow sounded very loaded, but Ashley was too pissed to be able to tell for sure.

'Last orders, gentlemen!' the barman called.

Chaz stood up. 'Let us retire to our makeshift boudoir. I bagsy the back seat.'

Weirdo, thought Ashley.

The tinny beep of Ashley's Rolex awoke him in the chill of a June dawn, his cheek freezing from where it had been pressed against the glass of the passenger window. There was a stream of cold dribble down his chin, his head was pounding and his bladder bursting.

With a groan, he heaved open the door and took a long, blissful piss behind a tree on the front lawn of Hetty Stinchcomb's opposite neighbour. He didn't remember how they had got there – presumably Chaz had located their prey's modern cul-de-sac and driven them there from the pub – but he supposed he was grateful that one of them had remained sober enough to do so.

With a small shake of his tackle and a quick gentle knee bend as he did up his flies, he went to climb back into the car. It was only then he noticed that the back seat was empty. No Chaz.

Puzzled, he looked around him, as though Chaz might randomly have lain down and chosen to sleep on the pavement instead. He climbed back into the car, sinking gratefully down into the leather seat still warm from his bulk. The keys were in the ignition, so he leaned across and switched on the engine to have heat and the company of the Radio 1 early-morning DJ.

He waited for an hour, wishing he'd had the forethought to buy a bottle of water and a sandwich. As far as he could recall, there had been no sustenance other than pork scratchings last night.

Chaz did not return. The first faint rumblings of concern were nagging at the back of Ashley's mind when, at 6.07 a.m., a flash of red rounding the corner into the cul-de-sac distracted him: the postman! At last!

Ashley leaped out of the car and lumbered towards the alarmed-looking man. 'Hi!' he said, then dropped his voice slightly in case Hetty Stinchcomb was an early riser. It was very quiet in the close.

'Hi,' he repeated, several tones lower, directing the words towards the postman's knobbly knees under khaki shorts, 'I need your help ...'

A mere seven minutes later and minus fifty quid from his wallet, Ashley returned jubilant to his car, the letter with its distinctive London South Television logo safely clutched in his paw.

'Thank fuck for that,' he said out loud, no longer caring if anyone heard him. It didn't matter now! His job was safe, and therefore so were his chances of promotion. This could henceforward be nothing more than an excellent tale with which to regale in the pub.

But where was Chaz?

Ashley decided he'd wait another half an hour and then Chaz would have to make his own way back to London. He couldn't imagine what had happened to him. Perhaps he'd pulled last night and had gone off on some sort of secret rendezvous with a bird? Ashley racked his brains, but even through the fog of his hangover, he didn't recall any suitable candidates.

Perhaps that sly bastard had left him in the car while he'd gone to stay with some previously unmentioned friend who lived nearby. He was probably tucked up in a comfy double bed in the local area, laughing at him, Ashley, having to sleep in the cold car, some sort of irritating payback for having played the prank in the first place.

That decided him. Fuck it – Chaz could make his own way back. Disgruntled, Ashley put the car into gear and drove off.

He didn't return to the office that day, preferring to heed the siren call of his own king-size and sleep off his Old Peculier headache.

The next morning he awoke feeling like a new man, optimism and energy coursing through his veins. Although he didn't know where it had come from, he had a sudden unshakeable certainty that the Head of Drama job would be his. Today was the day. He could visualise Innes-Hopkins summoning him to his office, shaking his hand, unstoppering the Scotch. He could almost taste the single malt burning triumphant on his tongue and see the extra zero on his bank balance.

He had not been at his desk long enough even to load up the *Secret of Monkey Island* when indeed Shirley did ring his extension to inform him that he had been summoned to Brian's office. *Here we go!* thought Ashley, rubbing his hands together with glee as he lumbered through the office.

He was so certain that Brian had good news that at first he totally failed to clock the atmosphere around him. It was only when he spotted a producer and his line-producer huddled together by the filing cabinets, weeping and clinging to each other, that he frowned, then assumed that they'd probably just discovered how far over budget they had gone.

Brian's door was closed and the blinds were pulled down. Ashley marched inside – and the smile immediately fell off his face as he was greeted, not by Brian with the congratulatory crystal tumblers and the decanter, but by two large unfamiliar strangers.

Brian sat behind his desk, a distant expression in his eyes.

'Come in, Ashley,' he said. 'These gentlemen are detectives who would like a word with you. They want to discuss ... this, which Shirley brought to my attention yesterday. I'm afraid I had no alternative than to call the police.'

He slid a sheet of paper across the desk towards Ashley as though it were radioactive. Ashley picked it up and read it. It was a message printed out of Chaz's draft email folder. Phrases jumped out at him: *'Ashley's been verbally abusing me for months ... desperate for that promotion, at any cost ... In case something happens to me ...'* and finally: *'He'll make it look like an accident ...'*

He sank into the nearest chair. Surely Chaz wasn't referring to *him*? He focused on the email in case he'd made a mistake, but, no, there it was, his name and all those damning accusations.

'Where is Chaz?' he asked the two detectives, unable to keep the quaver out of his voice.

'Charles Gest's body was discovered yesterday morning hanging from a tree in the woods near Winterbourne Prior in Wiltshire. We'd like you to accompany us to the station to answer a few questions as to your own whereabouts early yesterday...'

'Oh shit,' Ashley whispered.

Shirley watched through her curtain of hair as Ashley strode through the office to meet his fate. She already knew what Chaz had done, of course; she had known before anybody else.

She felt sad for Chaz – but she'd never have been able to dissuade him. The man wanted to die. Who was she to play God and try to stop him? He was going to die anyway, so he said. He'd been given six months. Cancer – a nasty, fast-growing untreatable one. Surely it was only humane to encourage him in his desire for a swift end at his own hands rather than an undignified, painful and lingering departure? She had done all she could to help and support him in the couple of weeks since his diagnosis and subsequent decision. The poor guy's wife had run off with her squash coach a few months earlier, so he had nobody else to confide in.

Then she had spotted Ashley's little addendum to the Hetty Stinchcomb letter and a plan had begun hardening in her brain, coiling round and round like a snail's shell, making her hug herself with excitement and anticipation. She knew that both Ashley and Chaz would do anything to get the letter back if it was sent – Hetty Stinchcomb would have shouted from the rafters for their dismissal and disgrace.

The only uncertainties were whether a kind sorting-office employee would help them retrieve the letter before it reached Winterbourne Prior, and then, of course, whether Chaz would have the guts to go through with his own plan. He had demurred to her on the phone that it was a mean stunt to play, to make Ashley the last person to see him alive, but Shirley merely reminded him that in their game of one-upmanship, this was surely the ultimate victory?

It was a win-win situation. Chaz would fulfil his final wish. Ashley, that foul-breathed lecherous animal, would get his comeuppance. Chaz wouldn't have wanted his death to result in a promotion for his twattish colleague! And – this was the bit that neither of them knew about – the third shortlisted candidate was an old friend of Shirley's, Nicolette, who had promised that if she got the Head of Drama job, her first task would be to give Shirley a promotion of her own, up to producer. It was the break Shirley had been waiting for.

So she had printed off the letter, folding it in thirds before she gave it to Chaz to sign so that he hadn't spotted Ashley's addition to it. When Chaz rang her from Fleet Services to get Hetty Stinchcomb's address, he told her he'd bought some rope and that he was going to do it soon, and how grateful he was for her understanding.

As before, she had not tried to dissuade him, just made the right sort of sympathetic noises. After he said his final tearful farewell, she had rushed back to the empty office, logged on to his computer and composed the draft email that she knew was now being discussed by Brian, Ashley and the two uniformed police officers.

She felt a tiny bit guilty. Not about Ashley, who deserved everything he got (well, Shirley thought, you had to be ruthless to work in television, everyone knew that. It was karma, that was all. He wouldn't be convicted of murder, as there was no hard evidence, but he'd definitely be out of the running for the job), but about poor Chaz dying alone at his own hands. She imagined him swinging in a silent forest, and for a brief second a lump sprang to her throat.

But then she thought with anticipation of her own imminent promotion. Nicolette would likely give her Chaz's actual job – and without having to have Ashley as a colleague! Brilliant, she thought.

She decided to go over to Nicolette's later to give her the good news that the competition was unexpectedly out of the running. She'd take that bottle of Dom Pérignon she had been saving for years, and they could have a premature celebration. Then she could go home and watch the concluding episode of *The Matchbook Murders* while reflecting on the fact that she would never again have to tolerate Ashley's meaty halitosis as he dictated letters and stared at her cleavage as she typed them up.

It's what Chaz would have wanted, she thought. She smiled to herself. *May he rest in peace.*

THE DAY OF THE DEAD

ALISON JOSEPH

The sea-washed bone fragments glistened against the blue forensic-issue glove.

'Vertebrae,' he said. 'Human.'

DI Berenice Killick looked at the mud-brown curl in the police sergeant's hand.

'Now we just need to find out who the poor bloke was,' he went on. 'The skull shows a blow to the head, but that tide has come in and out for some years since this poor chap was washed out to sea.'

The shingle beach glinted in the thin morning light, dotted here and there with crisp white-clad human forms. DS Ben Pask looked out to sea. 'Some poor guy fishing for herring. Scratching a living ... Maybe we'll find ID, threads of a jumper, a shoe if we're lucky. You on this case, Chief?'

Berenice shook her head. 'I was just passing. I've been given another shout. Missing person. A middle-aged woman wandered off from her home up the river there, hasn't been seen for a day or two.'

'Lucky you,' Ben said. 'You always get the sexy ones.'

Berenice raised an eyebrow. 'A missing woman? A nun at that.'

He smiled. 'Perhaps the boss thought it needed a woman's touch,' he said.

Berenice slumped into the car passenger seat.

'A woman's touch,' she said.

DS Mary Ashcroft put her foot down and the Corsa roared into life.

'You're the DI – you should have first call. It's your team out on the mudflats. You've got the DI nameplate on your office door now. So why did the chief super give the big case to a new boy?'

'Which answer do you want, Mary?'

'Which would you like? Race or gender?'

Berenice yawned. 'Can't we have a new one?'

Mary changed up a gear. 'Like what? Star sign? Musical taste? The fact we're from Yorkshire?'

'The super's always going on about wanting team players.'

'In my experience' – Mary put her foot down – 'being a team player depends on the team wanting you on it in the first place.'

Berenice gazed out of the window. The Kent marshland gave way to bare fields iced with autumn frost. 'You mean like at school,' she said. 'Netball...'

'Oh God. I was always last to be picked. The weedy white girl...' Mary laughed. 'Where we going, boss?'

Berenice checked her notes. 'St Margaret's Priory,' she said.

'A convent?'

'Where else would a nun disappear from?'

They drove in silence. A motorbike roared up behind them and accelerated into the distance ahead of them.

'You get his number, boss? He was doing at least a hundred.'

'I ain't no traffic cop. And in any case, we pull him over, a black woman and a white woman in an unmarked car, you in your pink fluffy coat looking about ten, me in this old grey duffle coat looking like your mum – he'd just laugh.'

'Hmmm.' Mary slowed as they reached the village. 'I don't look much younger than you.'

'That's because you ain't.'

'Two years is a lot at our age.'

'You'll soon catch up.'

Mary swerved the car into the convent drive and came to a halt.

Berenice got out of the car.

It was a neat, modern, suburban house, with neat, modern windows and a neat, clipped garden.

'Oh,' she said.

'What?' Mary stood beside her.

'I was thinking more...'

'Stone walls, gothic arches, the occasional ghost?'

'Exactly.' Berenice took a few steps towards the entrance. 'Except, I don't believe in ghosts.'

'At least there's this, boss.'

They paused in front of a statue, a Madonna and child carved in stone. The detail – the elaborate veil, the round-faced baby, the mother cradling her child with Victorian sentimentality – had survived the years, as if in defiance of the stark modernity of the buildings behind her.

The drive cut across the well-kept lawn. Beyond, a line of trees, all autumn reds and golds.

A white-robed nun appeared in the doorway and ushered them inside.

'It's just not like her,' Mother Patricia said. Tea had been served, and Berenice and Mary were now sitting with a group of five sisters, listening to descriptions of Sister Amelia, about how the community had realised she'd gone missing the day before, about how out of character it all was.

'We don't go far, usually. Into the village for errands, that sort of thing.'

'She liked her walk, didn't she? Up there, along by the river.'

'The mill race,' one of them said. 'She used to walk that way, up by the old canal lock. There's very deep water there...'

The room was brightly lit and lined with armchairs. A plain wooden cross hung on the white-painted walls.

Berenice addressed the small group. 'Did she seem happy?'

Glances flicked between them. 'Yes,' Mother Patricia said. 'As much as one can tell.'

'Who realised she'd gone?'

'Sister Abina, didn't you?'

The nun who spoke was younger than the others, dark-skinned, soft-voiced. She nodded. 'I went into her room, thinking she must be there – we hadn't seen her at chapel. And there was her habit laid out on the bed. Like the shedding of a skin.'

There was a brief silence.

'She was talking to a man,' the Mother Superior said.

'A man?'

'Yes. He came to the gate, asked for her. They had a long conversation. Then he went.'

'When was this?'

'About a week ago. And then she went. Some time yesterday. Just vanished.'

Berenice glanced at Mary.

'What did he look like?'

The nuns shuffled on their seats. 'Big,' one of them said.

'Scruffy,' said another. 'With a beard.'

'Lots of hair. Ginger hair,' Mother Patricia said. 'And a funny eye.'

'Funny in what way?' Berenice saw that Mary was making notes.

'Kind of drooping, half closed.'

'You must have got quite near,' Berenice said to her.

Mother Patricia looked down, then back up at her. 'Yes,' she said.

'Had she talked of leaving?'

There was a general shaking of heads.

'I mean, we all do, from time to time. But I hadn't heard her say such a thing for some time now. Well' – Mother Patricia got to her feet, followed by the others – 'do let us know if we can help any further.' She went to the door and turned to Berenice. 'It's a vocation, you see. It's not always a straightforward path. We make vows. Poverty, obedience –'

'You should try being a copper,' Berenice said.

There was laughter as the sisters filed out of the room.

Sister Abina led them back to the main entrance. Mary went ahead, her radio crackling messages.

'I hope she comes back,' Abina said. 'Finding her habit like that...' Her eyes welled with tears.

She placed her hand on the polished wood of the front door, then let it fall to her side. 'I think she'd stopped wanting to be here,' she said.

Berenice waited. Outside, the sunlight flickered through the trees.

'The statue.' Sister Abina waved her hand towards the front drive. 'The old statue of Our Lady. She'd taken to standing in front of it, crying.' She hesitated. 'She said something last week... about how it makes no difference, all of us sitting here praying all day. People don't usually say things like that unless there's a real problem.'

'My mother used to,' Berenice said.

'Your mother?'

'I had a brother, an older brother. He died as a child. She's never recovered.'

'She lost her faith?'

Berenice shook her head. 'That was the odd thing. She was convinced she'd see him in heaven. It was all she thought about, really, being reunited with him.'

'Even now?'

Berenice thought for a moment. She nodded. 'Yes. Even now.'

There was a chill in the corridor, a smell of cooking, bread perhaps. Somewhere a bell was ringing, a sombre tolling.

'Well' – Sister Abina's hand went to the door again – 'I hope you find her.' She opened the door, peering out into the chill October sunlight. 'Perhaps it's nothing at all. Perhaps she'll turn up and we'll all go on as if nothing's happened.' She reached out and shook Berenice's hand. 'God bless you, sister.'

Berenice walked back towards her car. The bell was still tolling. In the distance a white-clad figure flitted across the lawn, then passed out of sight.

The Madonna stared down at her. Berenice paused in front of it. She remembered her own mother after her brother's death, rocking, weeping, the voice that had sung so loudly in church, praising the Lord, now choked with grief.

Mary revved the car engine as Berenice joined her.

'What you thinking, boss?'

'I was wondering whether faith ever survives death.'

Mary sighed. 'He casts a long shadow, that brother of yours, doesn't he?'

'She'd light candles, my mother would. The day of the dead.'

'Tomorrow,' Mary said.

'It is?'

'Halloween tomorrow. When the boundary between the living and the dead gets thin.'

'She'll be lighting her candles, up in Leeds. Sitting by the window. Waiting for a sighting of him.'

'Tough call for you, boss. How old were you – nine, wasn't it? When he died?'

'Yeah.' Berenice fiddled with her coat. 'You don't get over it, really. My mother, she never got over it. But then you wouldn't, would you?'

'Even if you had another kid to look after?' Mary's voice had a hard edge. 'Like his little sister, for instance.'

Berenice looked out of the window. The statue stood staring, watching.

Mary put the car into gear. 'No wonder you refuse to believe in ghosts.'

Berenice sat alone in the imaging room. Scratchy images in black and white flicked up on the screen in front of her. She scrolled through them. 'Camera 201. 15.05. 15.10 ... 15.25 ...'

The canal towpath. A figure, medium height ... female.

She clicked back to it.

15.15. Quarter past three yesterday afternoon. A woman walking by the side of the canal. Where it crossed the river.

Camera 202... 15.20...

There she was again. An upright, purposeful look to her. Raincoat neatly belted. Sensible shoes. Wispy pale hair...

Camera 203. No sign.

Just the old lock gates, the crumbling Victorian brickwork...

'Any luck?'

Phil, imaging officer, put his head round the door. 'Ah, the old pumping station. I remember when the lock still worked. My dad used to talk about the boats coming through, carrying the fish inland.'

'I think I've found her.' Berenice clicked through the images.

He peered at the screen. Phil was pale-skinned and balding, with angular spectacles and a body toned by cycling. 'Yeah,' he said. Another glance at the screen. 'Doesn't help you now though.'

'It's a starting point at least.'

He nodded. 'All we can do. It's a mouse, not a magic wand.'

She laughed.

'I'm going to have to tell the chief that too. We've got the brother in, did you hear?'

'Which brother?'

'The bones washed up on the mudflats. Came to the front desk. Said his brother was out fishing, reported missing seven years ago. Bram Acland. It corresponds to all our reports. Just have to check the DNA.' He glanced at the images frozen on the screen. 'Missing people. They always leave a hole in people's lives.' He sighed. 'They worked together at Croney's yard, the brother said, the old shipwright's down by the lookout. It all answers the spec. Taped an interview an' all. The chief will want specifics. There won't be any. Just a poor sap who lost his brother seven years ago and got tired of waiting for the end of the story.'

He clicked the mouse. The screen went blank. Then a colour image, a man, hunched on a hard chair in the interview room; the background microphone hum.

'I'm just glad he turned up at last,' the man was saying. 'Seven years. Seven years, four months now. He'd go out fishing. Boat was found abandoned. We always thought he'd just drowned, out fishing.'

'There are signs of an injury...' The interviewing officer's voice. 'Did he have any enemies?'

The man shook his head. He looked weary, with a bushy beard, a loose jacket, straggling locks of hair. 'We lived quietly. He did his work, played his guitar. We used to run the shipwright's yard together, took it over from our dad. But when he vanished...' A break in his voice. 'I struggled on alone for a bit, but the trade died away. I gave up after a while. I've kept the yard on, doing bits of carpentry now, getting by, you know.' He lifted his face towards the camera. His eyes were tearful. One of them seemed half closed. 'I'm just glad to think of him at peace now.'

Phil clicked on pause. He turned to Berenice. 'He don't look guilty to me,' he said. 'If it was my brother washed up on the beach there, there'd be loads of suspects. And I'd be top of the list. But then he's a pillock. You ask anyone.'

'Good it's in colour.' Berenice nodded her head towards the screen.

'It is?'

'That ginger hair is distinctive.'

'Lot of it, given his age.' Phil ran his hand over his head. Berenice got to her feet.

'Good luck with the nun. Perhaps she fell in the canal. Too busy seeing visions of Jesus or something.'

Berenice didn't feel like laughing.

She went to her office. She thought about a white habit laid out neatly in an empty cell. She thought about those who went missing, leaving holes in people's lives. She thought about the nun's words: 'lots of hair, ginger hair – an eye, kind of drooping...'

She thought about dead brothers and the thin membrane between the living and the dead.

She turned to her screen and clicked on the files that Phil had now sent through. The scratchy black-and-white image, a woman on the canal towpath. A woman walking purposefully away.

What did Phil say? Croney's yard. Down by the old lookout.

A few clicks. A scribbled address.

Her office door with its detective-inspector nameplate shut behind her.

Team player, she thought.

Sometimes it worked better to be on your own.

Croney's yard was easy to find, if only because there was nothing else there. A tumbledown shed, its blue-painted woodwork faded to a lichen green, the tiles on the roof patched with bits of slate.

Her handcuffs clinked in her jacket pocket as she crossed the yard.

There was a smell of cigarettes and engine oil.

He was sitting on an upturned boat.

He looked up, blank-eyed. The same ginger hair. The same uneven gaze.

'DI Berenice Killick.' She flashed her card. 'Police. Sorry to hear they've found your brother,' she said.

'Yeah,' he said. His voice gave nothing away. He had a dried-up fragility in the lines of his face, the hunch of his shoulders. Above, a crow hopped to and fro on the uneven roof.

'Well.' He stubbed out his cigarette under his scuffed lace-up boot. 'He's been gone a while. You get used to it.'

'Do you?'

He looked up at her. A slight softening in his expression. A shrug, his gaze still fixed on her. 'You looking for something?'

'Yes,' she said. 'Actually I'm looking for Sister Amelia.'

His eyes flashed with recognition. 'So am I,' he said.

After that it was easy, she told the chief super on her return.

She'd sat down quietly on the boat, next to him.

'I'd give anything to find her,' he'd said. 'It's my fault she's gone.'

'It is?'

He'd put his head in his hands. Some moments passed. He'd raised his head, fished in his pockets, lit another cigarette.

He drew on it deeply. Berenice watched the curl of smoke against the chipped tiles of the roof. The crow had come to a standstill, eyeing them warily.

'We both loved her,' he said at last. 'Amelia.' He turned to her. 'If you'd seen her in those days…' His face softened. 'Music, dancing… she sang with Bram in his band.'

Another drag on his cigarette. 'She had long blonde hair. Beautiful hair.'

'Mr Acland,' she said, 'your brother had a head injury. Before he drowned.'

He shifted his weight, the ruin of the boat tilting beneath them. He faced her. 'Will you find her, do you think? Amelia. Please find her. It's because he's come to light. Because it's all come to light.'

'Did she love him?'

A shadow crossed his face. 'She chose the convent.'

The sun had gone in. The sky was heavy. A second crow landed on the roof, stepping tentatively around the first.

'Mr Acland –'

'Adam,' he said. 'No one uses my other name.'

'Adam,' she said, 'I'm thinking you know who killed your brother.'

He faced her. He got to his feet and lumbered towards the workshop. 'Look,' he said.

She followed him, her eyes adjusting to the shadows. She saw a workbench, a lathe, tools shiny with age.

He was holding something out to her. It was a small, curved wooden shape. She saw the warm brown of the wood, a hollow for an eye, a beak.

'A raven,' he said. 'For my brother. In the hope of seeing him again. It's unfinished, you see. Waiting for him to come back.'

She held the bird in her hand, admiring the lines of the woodgrain, the rough curve of its wings.

'Bit of a sideline,' he said. 'Goes with the carpentry work. The odd commission.'

The bird held her in its empty gaze. She handed it back to him. 'My brother died,' she said. 'When I was a kid.'

'Hauntings,' he said. 'They never go away.'

She looked up at him.

His eyes were fixed on hers. 'Stuck,' he said. 'The thin surface between the living and the dead. I haven't been able to move on.'

'Two brothers,' she said, 'loving the same woman.'

'Oldest story in the world,' he said.

'A blow to his head,' she said.

He turned suddenly away from her, paced back to the boat, and sat down heavily.

She followed, took her place beside him again, and waited. After a few moments he turned to look at her. 'Nowhere left to hide,' he said.

He stared up to the roof. The crows were silhouetted against the gathering clouds. He turned back to her. 'Are you going to arrest me, then?'

'I'm afraid I have to,' she said.

He sat beside her in the Audi. The engine purred under her feet.

'We both loved her,' he said. 'She chose him. I couldn't stand it…couldn't bear it. Rage, jealousy…I took him out in the boat, hit him over the head. He went over, went down…The sea was black, the darkness closing over his head…'

'And Amelia?'

'She never forgave me. I ruined her life. She went into the convent, said something at the time about being in a cell, how it would make no difference. I didn't see her again. Until…'

'Until last week?'

'I knew he'd washed up. I'd heard from the fishermen down there. Human bones.' He looked up at her. 'Please find her. It will have brought it all back to her. That's what scares me.'

They listened to the soft beat of the windscreen wipers against the late-afternoon rain.

He spoke again. 'When you find her – if you find her...' His hands twisted in his lap. He went on, 'I made her a carving all those years ago. When she went into the convent. A mother and child. In beech wood. Just small, like this.' He held his hands a few inches apart. 'I hope she kept it,' he said.

Detective Chief Superintendent Stuart Coles gazed out of the window. 'But you have to understand, Miss Killick – all this is just a story.'

'He's admitted it.' Berenice stared at his back, which was large and somehow clumsy, swathed in crumpled suiting.

The bright fluorescent light gave off an insect-like hum.

'You went alone,' he said. 'No observing of protocols.'

'I made an arrest,' she said. 'Sir,' she added.

He still had his back to her, leaning on the radiator, gazing down at the car park.

'That's all very well' – he turned slightly towards her, his wide pink face under its thatch of brown hair – 'but it's hardly going to work in court, is it? What we need is witnesses.'

She faced him, and for a moment his eyes locked with hers.

'I'll find you a witness,' she said.

In the dusk, the mill race seemed bottomless, a frothing depth of water, the rusted machinery looming over it. Beyond it, the pumping room, its old bricks glinting red in the light from a distant street lamp.

Berenice stared into the water.

I promised the chief a witness.

No good if she's down there.

Under her feet, the water surged and foamed.

A smell of woodsmoke.

A wisp from the old chimney.

Berenice picked her way across the narrow bridge. She pushed at the door, which hung half off its hinges.

She could see nothing. Only a smouldering glow in the old fireplace.

'Amelia?' Her voice soft in the damp air.

A shape, moving in the shadows.

'Adam,' Berenice said, 'he's admitted it all, to loving you, to killing his brother...'

'Who are you?' The voice was firm and clear.

'Berenice Killick,' she said. 'Police.'

'Police?' She stepped out of the darkness, her face white against the soot-charred walls. 'What did he say?'

'He's admitted to killing his brother. He's been arrested for murder.'

She was taller than she'd looked on the CCTV. Berenice took in the stately posture, her raincoat draped like an evening gown, her soft, once-blonde hair tied back.

Amelia gazed at Berenice for a long moment. The meagre sticks of wood shifted in the grate. She shook her head. 'So long ago,' she said. She settled on her makeshift bed, a pallet of wood, some damp blankets.

Berenice sat down next to her. 'You were there?'

She stared into the fire. Her face was illumined in the glow.

'You were there when Adam killed his brother?' Berenice said.

'No.' The word shot from her.

'You weren't there?'

'I was there. But Adam didn't kill him.' In the grate, a flame flickered into life.

'Adam loved you?'

A barely perceptible nod.

'And you loved Bram,' Berenice said.

A sigh. Of yearning. Of longing. 'Bram was the love of my life,' she said. 'Or so I thought.'

'A musician?'

She nodded. 'Wonderful times,' she said. 'We were so happy. So, so happy. Music, laughter, craziness...' She smiled, radiant with memories.

'So – Amelia – what changed?'

The light seemed to go out. She dropped her gaze. 'Everything changed. Everything.' She fell silent.

'Do you want to tell me more?'

She shook her head.

In Berenice's mind, an image of a woman standing before a statue of a mother and child, weeping...

'I was trying to imagine,' Berenice said, 'what would make someone that angry? It was quite a blow to the head. The marks on his skull...'

She didn't move.

'Men,' Berenice went on, 'they're trouble, aren't they? My last lover was a married man, promised to leave his wife, years it went on, and I believed him. Like a fool. Until I stopped. Being a fool, I mean.'

'I found a letter.' Her voice was low. 'In the studio...he was out. I'd just gone in to get something...It was there, on the desk. His writing. I read it...all about how he was waiting to be with her, how happy they'd be, how he loved only her...'

Berenice felt the icy chill of the room, despite the fire.

Again, the image of the mother with her child.

'Betrayal,' she said. 'Enough to make you so angry that you'd kill a man?'

'It was all I ever wanted. But Bram said the time wasn't right, not yet, later, if I made that sacrifice now, if I had faith ... So I ...'

'A baby,' Berenice breathed.

'He made me kill it.'

'An abortion?'

'I was raised a Catholic ... I'll never forgive myself. It was like a sore, spreading, suppurating. The pain so strong, so powerful ... in the end I couldn't contain it.'

They could hear the rush of water against the old lock gates.

'How?' Berenice broke the silence.

The cool grey eyes met hers. 'I'd taken him by surprise. Said I wanted to meet him on the shingle out by the boat. I was waiting. I'd chosen the rock carefully, could barely lift it myself. I brought it down hard, there' – her hand touched her own hair – 'on the back of his head. He kind of crumpled. I just stood there, listening to the breath go out of him. Out on the stones, a rock in my hand, blood ... so much blood ...'

Silence.

Then, 'And Adam?'

'Adam saved me.' Her voice was a monotone. She stared straight ahead, as if speaking to herself. 'He took control. He came running. He'd guessed what I was planning ... He found me. I was just standing there, staring down, the blood soaking into the mud, pools of red, bright, bright red ... He put me in his boat. He carried his brother, so heavy, doubled over ... Deadweight, they say, don't they?' She gave an empty smile. 'We went out beyond the headland there, the open sea. He pushed the body overboard. Left the fishing tackle as if Bram was in the middle of trying for a catch. He'd brought an inflatable; we paddled back to shore, disposed of the dinghy in a skip at the yard. "Tell no one," Adam said After that... he thought he'd win me. I tried... but all I could see was the blood... my own sinfulness. Every day since then I've confessed my sins. It doesn't make it go away.'

She breathed, in then out. 'And then, last week, he came to me and said the bones had come to light. I knew then that it was time to go. I always knew he'd come back somehow. I thought it would be a haunting, the spirit of him. But instead he came back as some gnarled old bones washed up on the shingle.' She raised her eyes to Berenice. 'A fraud, you see. That's what I am. To recite those words of goodness when all I am is evil.'

They sat, their thoughts drifting, entangled.

'They say you breathe water,' Sister Amelia said.

The birds outside had fallen silent.

'I've been dead for years,' she said. 'Another day won't make any difference.'

'You could always choose life,' Berenice said.

Amelia reached out and touched Berenice's jacket. 'Makes no difference to me now. It's too late. When I got rid of my baby, something in me died.'

She picked the handcuffs out of Berenice's pocket and held them between her fingers. 'I've always been locked away.' She held the handcuffs out to Berenice. 'It's a small step, to swap one cell for another.'

And now it was winter, and the trees were bare, the red and gold long gone. Amelia had pleaded guilty. At HQ, Berenice was praised until new cases came, new crimes to solve.

There was frost in the air as Berenice picked her way across the yard to Adam's workshop.

'How's it going?' she said.

'Look.' He held out the wooden raven. The wood glowed with polish, the eyes, now glass, were bright. 'Finished. In memory of Bram.'

'What will you do with it?'

He held it in the palm of his hand. 'Dunno,' he said.

'Amelia has your mother and child in her cell,' she said.

His face brightened at the name. 'You've seen her?'

'I visit from time to time.'

'How is she?'

'Happier, perhaps,' Berenice said. 'She said it's easier to have faith there. And the inmates are easier too.'

He laughed. 'She said that?'

They both looked at the raven. Adam held it out to her. 'For you,' he said. 'In memory of our brothers. To mark the thin boundary between this world and the next.'

She took the sculpture and stared down at it.

'See it as a Christmas present,' he said.

She smiled. 'It's a bit early for that.'

'Or a late Halloween present, then,' he said.

She cradled the bird in her hand. She looked up at him. 'It's lovely,' she said.

'It'll do,' he said.

THE SECRET INGREDIENT

HELEN SMITH

The steaming pile of rotting compost in the corner of Windmill Gardens was hot enough to incubate dragons' eggs. Emily Castles took a garden fork and drove the prongs deep, certain that nothing magical was hidden there. But once, long ago, she had been sure that dragons slept under autumn leaves swept into towering heaps by the gardeners in the local park. *At what age*, she wondered, *do we stop believing in magic?*

'Children start letting go of it at about eight years old,' her friend Dr Muriel told her. At twenty-six years old, Emily was about half Dr Muriel's age and twice as strong. They had both volunteered their help for the day at Windmill Gardens, the park that was home to Brixton's recently restored windmill. But Emily had worked harder, for longer. Dr Muriel was now sitting on a bench outside the café, in the spring sunshine, watching Emily tend to the flowers in the borders. Emily's bobbed brown hair was damp with sweat at the hairline. She attacked that compost heap with the determination of a land girl looking for a Nazi paratrooper hidden in a haystack during the Second World War.

Before taking a seat on the bench, Dr Muriel had explained, using a mathematical diagram drawn in the soil with the tip of her cane, that the amount of effort required to complete a task to a person's satisfaction was inversely proportional to that person's age. 'One doesn't become more efficient, one is simply satisfied with less.'

Emily stopped and wiped the sweat on her forehead with the back of her hand. 'Is that what wisdom is, then? You go from believing that anything is possible – even dragons sleeping in the local park – to being satisfied with very little?'

'You believed there were dragons because someone told you there were dragons – it made a nice story to pass the time during a walk in the park. At some point you started thinking for yourself, questioning what people told you. It was then that you stopped believing in dragons. We could say that wisdom comes from enjoying what is, not what might be.' But Dr Muriel was a philosophy professor, so she preferred asking questions to answering them. 'Here's one for you: you see a man pick a flower from a public park and put it in his lapel. Is he a thief or someone who appreciates beauty and wants to share it?'

Emily stopped forking and stood up to see what Dr Muriel was talking about. Gareth Crabbe, newly appointed poet-in-residence at Brixton Windmill, was striding towards them, a freshly plucked daffodil in the lapel of his long leather coat. His collar-length curly hair was bouncing in the spring sunshine and he was smiling eagerly, as if he expected a fond welcome.

'People never think they're the villain in a story,' Emily said.

'I think you're right about that. It's a shame we so seldom get the chance to ask the villain what motivates them.'

'We can ask this one.' Emily stuck the fork into the ground and watched Gareth approach. She was wearing her dark green work dungarees, her gardening utility belt and a sturdy pair of Wellington boots. Her mud-streaked arms were wiry but muscular. If woodland creatures had to elect a kick-ass heroine to protect the flowers of the earth, Emily would surely have made the shortlist.

'I'm wearing it because I'm Welsh,' Gareth said, joining Dr Muriel on the bench and taking a piece of the home-made fruitcake she offered. 'It's an emblem of my people.' This being Brixton, any allusion to cultural heritage usually shut down criticism.

'But why did you *take* it?' Emily asked. 'The flowers belong to everybody.'

'You may as well ask why I took a gulp of air!'

Emily hadn't spent back-breaking hours making *the air* look nice for visitors to the windmill. Dr Muriel tapped gently on Emily's leg with her Tupperware container of cake, offering her a piece to distract her from an argument, then handed round tea from a thermos flask. 'How's the work going, Gareth?'

'Not good, Muriel. The muse has left me.' He looked at the little wild birds chirruping in the trees nearby and then at the tip of the uppermost wooden sail on the windmill, as if he might see it perched there.

'I suppose a poem is like a recipe. There aren't many words that go into it, but you put a lot of thought into it. And if just one word is wrong, it's ruined.'

'Very wise, Muriel. And, may I say, whatever recipe you follow for this cake of yours, it's as delightful as any sonnet. The taste is excellent.'

Dr Muriel's cake had won first prize for two years running in the baking competition at the Lambeth Country Show, so he had said the right thing there. 'Thank you. It has a secret ingredient. All the best recipes have a secret ingredient, wouldn't you agree?'

'I don't know much about cake-making. Poetry now... I think the best poetry has a secret ingredient. You know, perhaps that's why I've been struggling. I thought it was something to do with money. Rich people say you shouldn't worry about money. Poor people worry all the time. I'm poor as dust, and I haven't been able to think of anything else for a while. I wake up and try to think of a poem and I think instead about how to pay the bills.' He paused and looked around to make sure they weren't being overheard. 'A man of my age shouldn't be sleeping on a camp bed in a café next to a windmill, but I depend for my livelihood on grant applications. I'm fifty years old and I'm living the same thrifty lifestyle I lived when I was a student. I've had this coat thirty years.'

'Oh, me too! I've worn this one so long the fashion's come back in. But that's only because I don't like shopping. I'm in the business of asking questions. That provides a steady income.'

But Gareth didn't want to talk about Dr Muriel's shopping habits or occupation; he was having an epiphany. 'This creative block isn't about outside forces. It's about me! I have been following the recipe and forgetting to include the secret ingredient. Thank you, Muriel!' And then, because he didn't want to seem like the sort of man who just talked about himself all the time, he brought the subject back round to cake. 'What *is* your secret ingredient, by the way?'

'People keep asking me what it is, but I will never reveal it! Lois who lives at number twenty-six is always dropping round on baking day, so I mislead her by leaving false clues for her to see, like half a block of lard or a tin of anchovies.

Emily's very good at solving mysteries, and even she doesn't know what it is.'

Of all the things Emily cared about, baking was low down on the list. But she was very fond of Dr Muriel, so she tried to look vexed.

'Ah.' Gareth reached for a second helping. 'Well, if you're good at solving mysteries, perhaps you ladies can help explain something strange that's been happening to me.'

'*Ladies* always sounds like a sign for a public toilet, don't you think?' Dr Muriel remarked pleasantly.

Gareth was keen to appease. 'You girls, then.'

Emily knew that her friend preferred the term 'women', but she wanted to hear about Gareth's mystery in case she could help solve it – she was a kind and helpful person, and after hearing that he was a poverty-stricken, creatively blocked, fifty-year-old mess, she had forgiven him for the daffodil. She offered him a refill from Dr Muriel's thermos and gestured for him to go on with his story.

Gareth politely declined the tea with a wave of his hand. He took a silver flask from the pocket of his coat and took a sip from it. 'I don't believe in magic, of course ...' But before he could tell them any more about it, he got a strange look on his face. Later Emily would describe it as something like fear, whereas Dr Muriel said it was horror. Whatever it was, Gareth stopped talking and looked out across the park. They turned to see what had caused this reaction. Was it human? Was it a magical creature that only Gareth could see?

It was Tia Langley, chair of Lambeth Council's Arts in the Parks committee. She was wearing purple because she had once read a poem that mentioned wearing it as an act of defiance. She took everything she read literally. And she was someone who liked to be defiant. She had left the house that morning determined to crush anything and everything that crossed her that day. Purple was her warrior outfit. Gareth was right to be afraid.

'I'll tell you the rest when we come out of the meeting,' he said, heading into Windmill Café, his temporary home for the tenure of the residency. 'I need to explain the arrangements for the poetry element of the gala that's been organised to celebrate the May Festival at the windmill.' He said it with the air of a man who has been called to explain why he decided to fake the moon landings.

Neighbours who had agreed to join the meeting included Lois Lippman, chair of the local Neighbourhood Watch and Social Committee; Derek Trees, a member of the committee who was keener on the neighbourhood watch part of it than the social events; and Victoria Blakely, a friend of Dr Muriel and Emily who ran local stage school Showstoppers. She had her youngest son with her, but she shooed him off to join in a no-rules kickabout game of football in the penned-off area next to the climbing frames.

Inside, the meeting had been set up with three rows of metal-and-canvas chairs facing the exhibition stands ('How flour is made', etc.) that created a temporary divide between the seating area and Gareth's sleeping accommodation. There was a large picture – about six feet high – of the two-hundred-year-old windmill in all its black-tarred, white-sailed beauty, painted in oils on board. Gareth's work.

'That's *very* good! We could always find work for you painting the sets at Showstoppers when you've finished living at the windmill,' said Victoria.

'I'm not actually living at the windmill,' said Gareth, sidestepping the offer of work, which Emily thought was rather clever: she suspected it might not involve getting paid. 'They've put me in here for the duration. I'll show you around.' They didn't have to walk very far. The café was a single-storey building; he could point to most of it. 'There's my bathroom: a sink and a toilet. Basic, but perfectly adequate for my needs. The windmill doesn't have any plumbing at all, which is why I can't stay there. You'll notice, by the way, that though the window in the bathroom opens and closes, there's no room for a man – or a woman' – this in deference to Dr Muriel's feminist sensibilities – 'to get in. There are windows at the front there, looking out on to the park and the playground beyond. But they're fixed. Similarly there are windows at the back.' He showed them a view on to the fenced-off land belonging to the waterworks, the generator for the café, the oil for the generator, and a short washing line with a pair of socks and a pair of underpants pegged up on it. 'But they don't open either. So there's just the door at the front. And I keep that locked.'

'Is that the mystery?' hissed Dr Muriel as they took their seats in the front row.

'It's part of it,' Gareth hissed back, 'but don't say anything – I don't want anyone to worry.' He meant that he didn't want Tia to know, which – having seen his look of fear (or was it horror?) – Dr Muriel and Emily instantly understood.

'Someone's been breaking in?' hissed Victoria, new to the story and glad to have some gossip to start off what was likely to be quite a tedious meeting. But because she was a trained actor and her sotto voce was meant to carry to the back of the stalls and up to the balcony, everyone heard her and turned round to look.

'What's been taken?' Tia called over.

'Not the bunting!' gasped Lois. She had spent three evenings sewing bunting from scraps of material got by cutting up old duvet covers and her daughters' summer dresses from last year. After losing her crown in the cake competition at Lambeth Country Fair and placing second for two years running, she was spending more time on crafts than baking these days.

'Nothing! Nothing was taken,' said Gareth.

'Vandals, is it?' Derek Trees was suddenly glad he'd come to the meeting. 'We'll have to mount a special patrol, then.' He strode to the windows at the front, assessing the threat from the boys playing football outside. 'We could use the garden forks and spades if challenged. I don't see how the police could object.'

'I'm not sure vigilantism is the answer,' said Dr Muriel.

'It's never the answer,' Victoria said firmly. 'Unless you're playing Scrabble.'

Apparently Derek didn't agree. He began his patrol immediately, checking windows and doors, peering into the bathroom, opening the fridge in the kitchen. Carton of apple juice in hand, sniffing it suspiciously, he called out to Gareth from the doorway. 'Why do they break in, then, if they don't take anything?'

'They... leave something.'

Wrinkled noses from the assembled company. It had been explained to them during a Neighbourhood Watch lecture that nervous burglars with loose bowels often left unpleasant 'deposits' that had to be dealt with during the clean-up process. Lois had rushed out and bought up the entire stock of Marigolds from the local Sainsbury's, just in case.

'Nothing like that!' Gareth told them. 'The intruder has been leaving poetry.'

Still they recoiled, as if breaking in and leaving poetry without consent was easily one of the worst things they could think of anyone doing, right up there with graffiti and defecation.

'There are some very funny people about.' Lois shuddered. 'No offence, Gareth. Make sure you double-lock your doors tonight, everybody.'

Derek got excited at the idea of everyone locked up in their homes for the night, in fear. 'You've kept the evidence? We could go to the police with it. Typed or handwritten – either way, we can catch the culprit.'

'It's more...ephemeral than that. Scraps of poetry. Words, phrases, prompts...Nothing that could be produced as evidence.'

Lois wrinkled her nose again. 'Ephemeral? Like what? Something that vanishes? Blood on a mirror that's gone when the sun comes up?'

Gareth gestured towards six tall glass jars lined up on the floor behind him. Each jar was about two feet tall and a foot in diameter and full of multicoloured plastic letters. 'It's here in the morning when I wake up, bits of poems made out of letters scattered on the floor. I clear it up after breakfast.'

In the murmuring that ensued, Tia took charge. 'If the project's at risk, we'll have to close it down.'

'It's not at risk!' bellowed Gareth. And then, more calmly, 'We're all set. We have twenty poems from the children's workshops I've been teaching.' He saw Lois's expression. 'Twenty *short* poems. The gala's going to be a lovely event.'

'And *your* poem?' Tia wanted to know. 'Because, Gareth, the funding of the residency is dependent on you producing an original poem, as you're only too aware. I have a cheque here. But...' She held the cheque up briefly, then tucked it away again in the folds of the nasty purple knitted thing she was wearing instead of a coat.

That look on Gareth's face again. Fear. Or horror. Anyway, a kind of agony, as plain to see as if it were written in a notebook, not splashed across his face: the financial worry of a man dependent on grants at the age of fifty and not having a poem to present in return for the next payment. The look belied the jauntiness of the daffodil in his lapel. Now Emily wished she had let him pick a whole bunch of them.

Gareth looked around him desperately. Dr Muriel smiled. Emily smiled. Victoria smiled. Lois smiled. Derek smiled. Tia folded her arms and waited.

'I have decided not to deliver a conventional text poem,' said Gareth.

'You won't be giving us...' Tia thought for a moment, seeking to define what a poem is or ought to be. 'You won't be giving us a piece of paper with words on it, then? You won't be giving us a poem?'

'I shall give you a poem,' Gareth declared. After all, the terms of his contract were clear on that point. 'But it won't be made of words.'

'Oh!' Victoria exclaimed. 'An *installation*?'

Gareth nodded cautiously. 'That's it.'

'*Such* a good way of reaching excluded young people and minorities. An installation will be *very* good for community outreach.' Victoria was a veteran of grant applications.

'All right...' said Tia. 'So long as it's a *thing* and I can see it or feel it. Don't go telling me it's a poem and I just have to believe in it and I'll see it. The council won't pay good money for something like that.' Tia had read her fairy tales. She was combative, but she wasn't an idiot. If somebody tried to sell her an invisible poem, she liked to think she would be one of the first to cry foul and get that person arrested for fraud – or at least blacklisted from every lucrative funding opportunity in the United Kingdom.

There was an awkward pause and then everyone stood up to leave. The moment to applaud had passed, somewhere between 'All right...' and 'The council won't pay good money...'

'There is just one more thing,' said Tia.

Everyone sat back down again.

'Your workshops with the children have been popular.'

'Transformative, some of them! Thank you. I've always been good with children. Poets and children, I think, see the world in a similar way. There's an innocence–'

Tia interrupted him. 'There have been reports of witchcraft.'

'I don't think that can be right,' said Gareth.

'Spells... Summoning spirits.'

'Ah! We call on the muse. It's not something external or magical. It's a gift that exists inside all of us. Look, I can show you. One of the boys outside will help me.'

'I could get Fox,' said Victoria. And then, because Derek Trees looked as if he might need to grab a garden spade: 'Fox is my son.'

Gareth held up his hand to stop her. 'There's a boy out there: Lenny. His journey has been quite remarkable. He was a difficult student. A difficult boy altogether, so I'd heard from his teachers. He came to the workshops reluctantly. But when he started writing poetry – when he was visited by the muse – it transformed him. I'm proud of what we have achieved together. His poem is one of the centrepieces of the gala.' Gareth stepped to the door and called Lenny inside.

Lenny was a boy of about ten years old, small for his age, with that cheeky expression children put up as a defence against being told off all the time. With Lenny's help, Gareth demonstrated the ceremony of summoning the muse. It was delivered with a flourish – like a magic show, but without any tricks.

'You're not alone when you write poetry,' said Gareth, opening his arms out wide and addressing the audience as if they were the children in his workshop. 'You have twenty-six little helpers...'

Lenny picked up one of the big glass jars, unscrewed the lid, and shook out a few hundred coloured plastic letters on to the floor to demonstrate this point.

'And you have your muse. The muse will only visit when you sit down and write. That's the signal. Begin to do the work and the work will begin... But what should you write about? That's what you're wondering.' Gareth took a notebook and pen from his jacket pocket and held them out to the boy. 'There *is* something you care about. Close your eyes now.'

Lenny's cheeky expression was replaced with a solemn look of concentration. He folded his arms across his chest, holding the notebook there, the pen sticking out of his fist. He closed his eyes.

Gareth's voice was very Welsh now, deep and musical. 'Let the name of the thing you care about come into your mind... Got it now? Got it? It can be just one word... something you care about. Put pen to paper and write about that.'

Lenny opened his eyes, sat down cross-legged next to Gareth, found a clean page in the notebook, and began to write.

'That's it?' asked Tia.

Gareth began to scoop the plastic letters back into the jar. 'That's how we summon the muse.'

Now there was applause. Now, surely, they could get up and leave!

'One more thing,' said Tia to Gareth. She might just be able to shut him down yet. 'What's *your* poem called? The one without words. I'll need to write it in the progress report when I get back to the office.'

Gareth scarcely hesitated. 'It's called ... *The Secret Ingredient.*'

Outside, Dr Muriel wanted to know if Gareth's installation would really be ready in two days.

'I think I can build it. It's sourcing some of the equipment that might be difficult. I need a camera and a small printer. I've got paint. And I should be able to get wood and wheels from a skip – everyone's mad for home improvement round here, aren't they?'

'It's really just like building a prop for a theatre show, isn't it?' Victoria believed that anything was possible if it could somehow be related back to the theatre. 'We have a photo booth we use at Showstoppers for end-of-term parties. You can use the mechanism from that if you put it back together when you've finished with it. Jump in the car with me now and we'll go and get it. Emily will help you. She can build anything. She's a whizz with set design.'

Gareth seemed excited about his new project, if a little overwhelmed by the scale of it. 'I'll need some recording equipment. Where can I get something like that?'

'Church halls or charity shops,' said Victoria, a regular nuisance at both. 'Fox! Come on. We're going now.'

Lois waited until Victoria and Gareth were out of ear-shot. 'I'm glad you're helping out, Emily. It will be good to have someone in situ in case the intruder strikes again. I agree with Derek that we should think about putting together a patrol.'

'I don't think we'll need a patrol,' said Emily. 'Gareth won't come to any harm.'

'Don't tell me you've already solved this one!' said Dr Muriel proudly.

Emily grinned. 'I think so.'

Derek seemed disappointed. 'Was it him? He did it himself ... maybe without knowing what he was up to? He drinks, you know. The apple juice in the kitchen wasn't apple juice, if you know what I mean.'

'I'd like to think it was a poltergeist,' said Lois, unexpectedly revealing more about herself than she realised. 'But that ceremony wasn't very powerful, was it? I couldn't see anyone summoning something evil with that by mistake. Maybe it was blackmail?'

Dr Muriel wasn't impressed by this suggestion. 'What kind of blackmailer threatens a man with no money? What do you say, Emily? Poltergeist, blackmailer, burglar, vandal, or the deranged activities of Gareth's unconscious, drunken mind?'

Emily enjoyed gardening, mysteries and making things – which was fortunate; otherwise she might have been irritated by all the duties she'd been volunteered for in the past twenty minutes. But of all these activities, the one she enjoyed the most was solving puzzles. She thought she'd solved this one and it made her happy. 'I'm sure it was a real person.'

Lois looked from Emily to Dr Muriel to Derek, as if daring them to admit their involvement. 'It's someone with a key! That's it, isn't it?'

'Gareth's the only one with a key,' grumbled Derek.

'What about that Tia woman from the council?'

'Surely it can't be Tia!' Dr Muriel said. 'Are you going to give us a clue, Emily?'

'Do you remember what we said earlier – that no one ever thinks they're the villain in a story? That's all I can give you for now. I need to test my theory about the intruder while I'm helping Gareth over the next few days. If I'm right, I'll tell you at the festival on Saturday.'

Over the next day and a half, Emily varnished, painted, hammered, sawed and sanded. She visited skips and charity shops. She made enquiries at church halls. She and Gareth worked hard, Lenny at their side. While they worked, they talked about poetry – and mysteries. In particular, they talked about the poetry that had mysteriously appeared during Gareth's residency.

'So all day long, you'd worry about poetry? You'd think you'd lost your muse and you'd never write again. And then overnight, someone would visit and leave you a poem. The question is who. If they existed, I'd say it was elves.'

Lenny and Gareth agreed that elves was a good answer, though not the right one.

'So if we don't know who, we could start with why. I'd say it was someone trying to help you.'

Lenny and Gareth agreed.

'As for how, the only way in is that little window in the bathroom. If there's only one answer to a question, that has to be the right one. So let's stick with that for now.'

'Perhaps this is one mystery that will never be solved,' said Gareth. Lenny agreed.

The only other thing they talked about a lot was the weather. If it was sunny, the festival was more likely to be a success. If it rained, on the other hand...

On Saturday when they woke up, the sun was shining. They had the poetry machine finished by mid-morning, just as the local businesses arrived to set up food stalls in Windmill Gardens. Along with noodles, burgers, pulled pork, jerk chicken, curry and hotdogs, there was to be a bar serving beer from the Brixton Brewery, and a tea table that would be set with sandwiches and cakes made from flour milled at the windmill.

Lois arrived early to put up the bunting. When she saw the installation, she said it was the most beautiful poem she had ever seen.

Even Tia seemed impressed. 'What time does it open? I can tick you off my list as soon as I see how it works.'

The festival was to be launched officially at one o'clock with music from the Mill Street Jazz Band. Members of the public could sample the food, buy freshly milled flour, and enjoy free tours of the windmill, going one at a time up the winding wooden stairs to admire the machinery and imagine a time when Brixton was considered part of the countryside. *The Secret Ingredient* poetry installation would be open for the duration of the festival.

That wasn't quite soon enough for Tia. 'I've got to get to Vauxhall. We've had reports of an allergic reaction to the latex in an exhibit at the Pleasure Gardens.'

Gareth offered to give her a preview of how it worked. He asked Lenny to do the honours as Lois joined Emily and Tia to watch.

It was a brightly painted wooden wagon on wheels, about six feet high and eight feet long, sturdy but slightly off-kilter, as if someone was recalling it from a dream. On one side there was a booth with a lit-up mirror, like the mirror in a starlet's dressing room, and a stool underneath it.

A sign below the mirror said:

There is a secret ingredient in poetry. Press the button and tell me what you think it is. Use just one word to explain it.

Lenny sat on the stool. He pressed the button and whispered into the mirror. A flash went off. It could have seemed like the flash from a magic wand if you wanted to believe that was what it was.

'Of course,' said Gareth, 'we'll get some swear words – from the parents mostly.'

Go to the next booth and wait.

Lenny walked to the booth at the other end of the wagon and waited.

The sign above a dispensing tray at the next booth said:

The secret ingredient is...

After about half a minute or less, a thick, square piece of paper fell into the tray. It was a photo-booth picture of Lenny staring solemnly into the mirror. At the top of the picture it said: *The secret ingredient is...* And underneath, in case the message wasn't obvious enough, it said: *You.*

Lenny picked up the picture and looked at it, pleased.

Go around to the other side of the wagon and you will learn what you should write your next poem about. It will be something important to you.

From behind the booth on the other side of the wagon, there was the sound of a small printer whirring. There was a tray to catch whatever instruction it should dispense. Presently it spat out a tile with one word printed on it. Lenny snatched it up and looked at it. He smiled. They called out to him to let them see it, but he wouldn't show it to them.

With a flourish, Tia took a handwritten list from her pocket and crossed off the first item on it. She had only taken two paces in the direction of the exit when she stopped and turned. 'There is just one more thing.'

Of course there was.

'If you discover who's been breaking into council property, will you let me know? I have to report them to the proper authorities.'

They promised they would.

'What a splendid contraption!' Dr Muriel exclaimed as she joined them. 'Will you let me have a go later if the queues aren't too long?'

'I think children should take priority,' said Lois.

'It would be nice to let grown-ups try, too,' said Gareth. 'There's something *confessional* about whispering into a mirror in a magical booth, isn't there? We should get some interesting results.'

Lois seemed excited by this. 'Come on, Muriel! The punters aren't here yet. There's plenty of time for you to try the machine. I can talk you through it.'

Emily watched, amused, as her friend took her place on the stool. She had a feeling she knew how this would play out.

Lois positioned herself with her back to the machine, obscuring the printed instructions on the wagon as she bent to explain to Dr Muriel what she should do. Dr Muriel leaned forward and whispered into the mirror. She chuckled as the picture of herself appeared at the next booth. 'Marvellous! And so true.'

When they got to the dispensing tray, Lois made a grab for the printed tile as it fell and…yes! Emily was sure she opened her hand and peeped at it before handing it over.

Lois left them abruptly. She said she felt that the bunting between the café and the windmill wasn't hung quite right, and no, she didn't need any help, thank you. She knew her way up and down a stepladder. Emily and Dr Muriel walked over to join Gareth and Lenny sitting side by side on a bench next to the tea table, both scribbling furiously in their notebooks.

Dr Muriel beamed at Gareth. 'The muse has returned at last?'

A sheepish look. 'Victoria has given me some tips about how to fill in my next grant application ... I need to get them down before I forget.' Another sheepish look. 'Something else before I forget.' He lifted up the tablecloth draped over the tea table to reveal what looked like a sack of onions hidden underneath it. 'Daffodils; I'll help you plant them, Emily. I wanted to thank you for helping me with the poetry installation. I couldn't have done it without you.'

'It's a very clever machine,' said Dr Muriel.

'Yes!' Emily was proud of the work they'd done. 'You get the child to say the thing that they think is the secret ingredient, but they learn that *they* are the secret ingredient. When they receive the prompt to write the poem, they're told it's something that's important to them ... and it is, because it's the word they whispered at the beginning.'

Gareth nodded. 'To the younger ones, it will seem as if the wagon is powered by a touch of magic.'

'And what about you?' Emily asked her friend. 'Did you tell it your secret ingredient?'

Dr Muriel opened her hand to show the printed tile she had received from the machine: *Anchovies.*

Emily laughed. Then she looked thoughtful. 'Do you ever wish you still believed in magic?'

Dr Muriel grinned. 'What makes you think I don't? All *this* tells you is that, if magic exists, I have learned to stay one step ahead of it.'

As visitors began to arrive and the jazz band began to play, Gareth and Lenny packed up their notebooks and took their places by the poetry machine, ready to guide people through the installation.

'Do we have confirmation of the identity of the intruder?' Dr Muriel asked Emily.

'If your life had been transformed by poetry, and you saw that the person who had helped you was struggling, what would you do?'

'I think I might want to muster "twenty-six little helpers" to try to trigger the appearance of the muse. If I knew where to find them. But how to get to them if I didn't have a key?'

'Well, if your home life was neglectful, so that you were allowed to wander around at night unsupervised, and you were malnourished and scrawny enough to clamber in and out of bathroom windows, you might not need a key.'

'Ah. I see.' Dr Muriel looked over at the poetry installation. 'We don't know anyone who fits that description, do we?'

'My best guess is that it was elves,' said Emily.

'That's a very good guess, under the circumstances,' her friend agreed.

WITCH

KATE MEDINA

The little boy sat by the side of the road and gazed through eyes unfocused by months of hunger at the dusty stream of aged motorbikes and cars trundling past him into the centre of town. He had been here before – perhaps. It all looked the same to him now. The endless streets that he had walked, the hours he had spent scavenging for food, fighting the stray dogs for scraps tossed from car windows or dropped by passers-by.

When had he been left? How long ago now? He didn't know. Time was meaningless to him.

What he did remember, faintly, the after-image on a negative, was following his mother out of their hut, tempted by fried, sweet plantain, a delicacy, the smell too tantalising to resist. She had held his hand, speaking calming words without looking at him. Talked and walked, holding his hand tight, pulling him along, further and further, her grip iron when his legs grew tired and he tried to yank away, whining to be taken home.

His bed was the cold gutter, and at night he curled tight into a ball as he had learned from the dogs, closed his eyes and imagined that he was back at home with his brothers and sister, he, the youngest, lying spooned against his sister's warm body. She would stroke his hair and sing to him until he was almost asleep and then thread her thin arms around his body and hold him tight, whispering the song into his ear, her voice fading as he lulled into unconsciousness. Now, staring at the cars and motorbikes, he tried to imagine the warmth of her touch. But he was too bone-deep weary, too starved to imagine anything. His mind refused to take him home, refused to take him anywhere. It just left him here, discarded by the side of this dusty road, with his aching belly, the pain in his skeletal frame and his loneliness.

His mother had stopped, finally, and wrenched her hand from his. He had reached up for the plantain, but she had held it high above his head, laughing as he stretched and wobbled on tiptoes. Sliding the plantain into her own mouth, she bent down so that she was level with him, held his gaze and smiled as she chewed.

When she had turned and walked away, he had run after her. But he was not yet two years old, and her legs were long and strong from walking to the well twice a day, from eating food that she had denied him. He ran and ran until he could run no more. Finally he stopped, exhausted, swaying on legs made pigeon thin and donkey bowed through neglect. He willed his feet to move, one of them to move, just one step, to follow his mother home, but however hard he tried to focus on his toes, he couldn't get them to obey. Looking up from his Judas feet, he watched his mother's form fading into the distance. He thought that she would look back, but she didn't. Not once.

Sometimes he tried to bring her face to mind. His father's. The faces of his four brothers and sister. But they were nothing now, as insubstantial as the dusty air around him.

The little boy sensed, suddenly, that he was no longer alone. Lifting his head, he looked up at the faces ringed around him. The blonde woman in their midst had drawn a crowd.

The little boy, unused to human company, was frightened. Struggling to his feet, he tried to run – he didn't know where, just anywhere, away – but legs as thick as fence posts were corralling him into a tight circle. Spinning in terror, he caught his heel on a stone and toppled backwards, landing hard on his bottom in the dirt. Pain ratcheted up through his broken body, jarring his head, oversized and unwieldy now on his tiny, rail-thin frame. But he didn't cry. Couldn't cry.

At first he had cried, but no one had come. Worse, he had been kicked. Kicked off his feet into the dirt like one of the starving dogs he fought against for scraps at the rubbish dump. Kicked by adults who knew exactly why he had been abandoned, when he did not. Those same adults who ringed him now, drawn not by him, but by the power of this woman, with eyes the colour of the clearest sky and hair as bright as the sun right in the middle of the day when it burnt his skin with its fierce energy. From behind, unseen hands hooked under his arms and lifted him to his feet.

He was full of fear. Fear at the unaccustomed attention, at how these people might hurt him. But he was more fearful now of being alone. He had been alone for too long.

The woman was holding out a plastic bottle of water. It had been so long since anyone had shown him kindness that he didn't understand that she was offering it to him.

'Take it.' Her voice was gentle. 'Take it. Drink.'

The little boy looked at her with huge dark eyes, tears making shiny tracks through the dirt on his cheeks.

'Mummy,' he whispered.

He clung to the bottle, holding it to his mouth, feeling the cool water run over his lips and fill his mouth. He coughed at first, choking on his sheer desperation to drink, on his greed.

The woman laughed. 'Slowly,' she said. 'You can drink as much as you want.'

She held the bottle for him with one hand, tilting it, controlling the flow, stroking his back gently with her other hand, talking to him, soothing words whose tone he understood. He didn't want to close his eyes, fearing that when he opened them again she would be gone.

'Mummy,' he whispered again.

The woman smiled. 'No, sweetheart. I'm not your mummy, but I will look after you.'

She had a kind face. But her blue eyes were bright and angry, and when he looked up at her, she dipped her head and looked away. He started to shake again, thinking that a kick or a slap was coming. Or worse, that she would stand and walk away, taking the crowd with her, leaving him alone again with his hunger and his fear and his aching loneliness.

The woman put the bottle down, reached out and pulled him gently against her.

'You're safe now,' she murmured, her lips moving against his cheek.

Pulling a blanket from her bag, she wrapped it around him. The little boy felt the soft wool slide over his skin. He could smell the laundry scent of the blanket, the perfume of the woman, and feel her heart beating against his chest through the wool. She kissed his forehead and held him tighter, lifting him off his feet and wrapping him in her arms. Her arms were strong and he hadn't been held, cuddled, for longer than he could remember. It felt so good that he started to cry, great sucking sobs that felt as if they came all the way up from the soles of his feet.

'Don't cry,' the woman said softly. 'There's no need to cry. Not now, not ever again.'

The little boy tried to smile through his tears, but he couldn't. Misery was so much a part of who he was that he couldn't see beyond it any more.

'What is your name?' she asked.

The little boy didn't answer, couldn't answer. He had been driven from his family home at the age of twenty-two months, barely talking. He hadn't heard his name spoken in so long that he had forgotten what he was called. Fresh tears sprang to his eyes. He felt desperate. Utterly desperate for this woman to like him, to hold him, to keep him with her.

The woman wiped away his tears with the soft tip of her finger.

'Hope,' she murmured. 'I will call you Hope.'

Note:

This story is the fictionalised account of a real-life incident that occurred in Nigeria in 2016, in which a two-year-old boy, who had been cast from his home because his family believed that he was a witch, was rescued from the streets by Anja Ringgren Loven, founder of African Children's Aid Education and Development Foundation, a charity that helps children who have been labelled as witches and expelled from their communities.

STEVIE

D.E. MEREDITH

M y name is Hope Kellaway.
Being Mrs Harrison was complicated, difficult from the very beginning.

But I'm back here where I think he wants me to be. On the same bend of the river, under the same shadow of the exact same tree, a raddled sycamore, but the revellers are all gone, the disco beat faded, the balloons washed away like flotsam.

Oh, Stevie.

Even saying his name makes me go weak at the knees and makes the air around me like I can't breathe. How long has it been? How many nights without him? Time seems to have compressed into nothing. If I close my eyes, I can still taste the salt of his mouth, feel the warmth of his belly, the nib of his tongue and the click of his teeth against mine.

But I'm not here to tell you about Stevie at all, or those hands they used to restrain me. The police pulling me away as they hauled his body out down on the riverbank, where seagulls skirled overhead as I leaned down to see nothing but brown skin, brown sodden clothes, brown sodden everything, like Stevie had been rolled in dirt for a thousand years or been dragged through a subterranean stream, except for the bright red nylon rope that tainted his neck. A neck I had kissed, bitten; a neck I had nuzzled against when it got too cold or too dark. Ligature marks, I later heard the police surgeon call them when we got to the morgue and a nice WPC asked if I'd like a cup of tea. I could have thrown it at her, milk, three sugars and all.

I'd been away a week on some bloody conference or other when the shit hit the fan and Stevie decided to jump.

On the phone I'd said to him, when he tried to explain what he'd been working on, 'I'm really sorry, Stevie, but I can't talk about this now. There's a briefing with the ministers in half an hour. I've got tons to do, a paper to write, you know the score.'

'For fuck's sake, Hope. There's something kicking off right here, right under our noses, whereas Brussels is full of corruption, Eurocrats, bullshit...'

'Listen, Stevie. You understand the pressure I'm under. You know what I'm up against. You know what it's like. Pressure, pressure, pressure. Everything has to be done yesterday, and it's driving me crazy.'

I could hear him breathing on the other end of the phone, how angry he was, how pumped up. He told me he was working on something *real*. I got the inference but didn't react as he rattled on about chemicals, a spillage, the rats with two heads. How toxins had been dumped in the river at night, though he didn't have any proof, no hard facts, not yet, but that he was close, very close to the truth.

'Are you even listening, Hope?'

'Of course,' I'd said with a sigh, looking at my nails, biting my lower lip the way I always did when I was lying.

Stevie meanwhile was rambling, in that crazy way of his, about how the fish in the Thames were lit up and glowing, the fishermen said; how their innards, as well as their scales, were Day-Glo blue, like alien aquatics in some sort of under-water sci-fi film. And how the hell did that happen, Hope? And how he was going to show the world we'd all been sold down the river. How all the measures, safety checks and laws meant nothing versus politics and money. Greed. And how he hoped we weren't thinking about getting pregnant any-time soon because we lived on the river, that self-same river that ran like an arterial vein through this city, but was less like blood keeping organs alive and more like a toxic stream of malignant tumours.

I'd had enough at that point. The thing about the preg-nancy brought tears to my eyes, so I cut him off. 'For fuck's sake, Stevie, get a grip.'

But he wouldn't let it go. And as someone else lifted my hair up from the nape of my neck and blew very softly on my skin, he said something about how I needed to support him. 'You're supposed to be my wife, after all,' was what he said, how I was all show these days, how I needed to put my ambitions aside. How I needed to come back to him, to us, was how he put it. How if I did that, we could live a different sort of life.

He didn't know then that I already was. How the tongue on the top of my neck was persistent and so was the hand creeping round and unbuttoning one mother-of-pearl but-ton, then another, then another, and how my breath was almost gone as I told him, 'I can't do this, not now,' was all I said. 'Jesus...'

'Jesus? Is that all you've got to say. I used to admire you, Hope. Think you and I were on the same side. But listen, I'm sorry. I don't mean any of that. I need your help. Now more than ever. I need you to get some data for me the next time you're with your government friends. You see, I've been work-ing on this investigation and I just need you to help me.'

Then he said something I couldn't really hear, didn't want to hear because I was exposed, so exposed, more exposed than I'd ever been in my life, as I said, 'Listen, Mike just walked in. Seriously, I've got to go.'

He couldn't see my face, what I was doing, because I was a thousand miles away in a hotel room, lying my head off, and those were the last words we ever spoke together.

I let him come over about an hour ago, I guess because I was scared. Alone. Haunted by old memories, haunted by what happened with Stevie.

He knocked on the door. I opened it and offered the inspector a chair, and we settled ourselves down in the snug of the hold. He took the battered red velvet chair with my blessing, and I took Stevie's favourite, the faded old yellow one, and I could hear, but not see, a swan's wings pounding a rhythm as it rushed across the water.

Despite the hour, the inspector was dressed all natty in a suit, a pinstriped waistcoat, a white shirt, solid gold cuf-flinks and a designer watch peeking out from the cuffs, say-ing loud and clear that he meant business, serious business.

I cleared my throat. 'Look, it's late. I'm tired. Do you mind if I just call you Ray?'

He smiled right back at me, licking his pencil, ready for whatever I was going to tell him, just me and him together as if he had all night to listen. Despite the suit, he looked relaxed as he slumped further into the chair, which smelt of old mothballs and cats. 'Of course you can, Hope. In fact, I prefer it that way.'

Trust is a dangerous thing.

I should have learned that a long time ago, because I was not some ingénue, some silly young thing. I was thirty-five and I had a serious job once, a husband, ambitions, dreams, a *life*. So I hesitated and sipped my coffee, which was strong and making me even more jittery. I hadn't slept for over a week. Longer maybe, who knew, but this man looked kind. Deep wrinkles at the corners of nut-brown eyes, a full mouth, clean shaven even at this ungodly hour, and his scent was fresh and expensive, suggesting to me the three key things I always looked for in a confidant – wisdom, understanding and empathy.

Like Stevie used to be.

Of course I wasn't stupid, and it occurred to me that Ray's night-time visit was unusual, together with the fact he'd come here on his own this time. No PC at his side to do that good cop, bad cop thing he seemed so enamoured of, and not even a two-way radio hanging from his belt, but he did have a small silver gun. I saw it in my peripheral vision as he shrugged off his coat. Cashmere camel, no doubt about it; it was Prada. I saw the label as he hung it on a hook next to Stevie's old parka.

And it occurred to me, for a cop, this wasn't right. It was a long way from right. The look of him, the smell of him, the time of his visit, his whole attitude. His sense of entitlement. Like he owned a piece of this boat and a little piece of me already.

All of which should have sent a warning sign telling me to be careful because I didn't know who he really was or what he really wanted. And the last few times we'd met, dinner and so forth, at Stevie's favourite pub, Ray had kept on and on, fishing, asking about what Stevie had been working on just before he died, if he'd seemed afraid of anybody or worried about anything.

You say he was a campaigner for an environmental lobby, right?

Your point being ...

All part of our ongoing enquiry, Hope.

You always do this for a suicide? Really?

Not always, but, well... you're a nice girl, you've been through a lot, and I'm a nice guy and...

He repeated the whole thing again as he sat opposite me, kicking off his loafers, which was weird, very weird, making himself at home. I was tired, so tired, too tired to argue. Instead I threw caution to the wind and decided that Inspector Ray was who he said he was. Someone who could illuminate truth. And I needed support, a friend, someone to talk to.

You see, ever since I came here, after Stevie died, I'd felt anxious all the time, but I didn't know why. Take tonight, for example, just before Ray came. I'd been skulking about with Stevie's hat on, listening to his playlist on my iPod, my nervous fingers tweeting people I didn't really care about but I'd promised I'd contact in honour of Stevie... campaigns about social mismanagement, government cover-ups, scandals, money laundering, that sort of thing. But when the music ended, I lifted my fingers from the keys and I felt as if someone was standing behind me, very quietly, just waiting for me to turn around.

Twice I twisted in Stevie's chair and said to the empty cabin, 'Who are you? What do you want?' And the presence wasn't benign. I knew it wished me ill; most of all I knew, whatever I'd done in the past, that he'd loved me to the end, and I knew this presence, whatever I was feeling, call it an impression, it wasn't my Stevie.

But I also I knew I wasn't safe any more. Over the last month or so I'd been given some warnings, parochial warnings... a bit of glass rammed into my bike wheels, dead rats left on the jetty, daubs of red paint on the portholes, a dog turd left on the welcome mat, that sort of thing... a note that said *BITCH*. But I didn't want to leave here. Not any time soon.

You see, Stevie had told me that this little piece of river meant the world to him, held a special place in his heart, which was why I didn't hesitate, didn't even think about it, coming back here, I mean. The second the lilies turned brown, his body was in the ground, I gave up my job and came here. Friends' misplaced phrases still ringing in my ears – *You'll get over this, Hope. Leave that shit alone. His business not yours. You need to move on with your life.*

But I couldn't. I was sick with grief at the time and I longed to be near him. I wanted to breathe the same air, run my fingers across the places he'd been, caress my face with his clothes, take them out, put them on, snuggle into bed, pull the duvet over my head, turn to the wall, and tell the world to go fuck itself.

Suffice it to say, I needed solace, and when Stevie was still alive, he had needed it too, maybe more than I ever knew. We used to come to this boat together on the weekends just to chill out, renaming it the minute we saw it, from something silly like the *Water Goddess* to the *Contented S.O.L.E.* – like the fish, geddit? We thought it was funny and laughed our heads off when Stevie lifted me over the threshold, Mr and Mrs Stevie, as he laid me down that first night and we talked about the children we'd have, how together we'd save the world, against the wash of the river, the loveliest sound to fall asleep to.

'Hope? Are you with me, Hope?'

What the hell? I looked up. I must have drifted off or zoned out. I did that a lot these days, so I apologised to Ray, who was still sitting there opposite me – Mister Serious Crime Detective.

And then he said, for he had such empathy for sorrow and death, 'Hope, if this hurts you...? I know it's hard to speak about Stevie, and I'm sorry I called on you so late. I'll come back tomorrow?'

I shook my head. I felt a tear, hot on my skin. The inspector leaned forward, dabbed my tear away, and as I put my hand on his, I saw the silk kerchief from Liberty's and I wondered – a nanosecond, no more – if maybe he was gay. That would explain a lot. Those tidy ways of his, his sharp, angular shape and that wet black rubber look he went for when he was trawling for 'floaters' – wasn't that what the professionals called them? I learned that from one of Ray's ex-colleagues, who was upriver in Wapping these days. That was where the search-and-rescue teams, the MPU, the river police, were officially based – the dead-body investigators like Ray, who apparently was some kind of world expert on organised crime, till things went a bit awry for him too.

Cancer. A dead spouse. Accusations from colleagues about not playing by the rules, never doing things by the book, misdemeanours, kickbacks (not proven) and other people's wives. A bit of a temper too.

You see, Ray didn't know this yet, but he wasn't the only detective. I used to do a job like Stevie's once upon a time – undercover investigator – and it took one to know one, I guess... liars, dissemblers and bad news cases.

With my hand resting in his, the inspector pressed my fingers, leaning so far forward we could almost kiss. 'Hope,' he murmured.

'Please, Ray, don't do that. Not yet. Just do me a favour and listen. Someone wants to do me harm. Skulking about there on the towpath. Throwing pebbles at the porthole. Making weird sounds. Whispers like it's a dead man. Maybe it's what you say it is, the wind over the water, but I don't think so. I think someone's trying to frighten me. Trying to make me leave here. Maybe it's just a local thing. There was some dispute with neighbours over this mooring, but that was yonks ago. Stevie told me it was all sorted out way back when.'

I shrugged at him. He lit a cigarette, smiled, and it struck me, there and then, how rare his smile was. Quite beautiful. Like Stevie's used to be.

'Maybe it's to do with Stevie? What he was working on?'

I felt a twist in my stomach. 'I'm scared, Ray. I'm not someone who scares easily, but I can't seem to find the wherewithal to pull myself together and shake off this feeling, like I'm being watched. Ever since I came here. Ever since –'

His voice was suddenly sharp, 'Are you sure he didn't give you anything before he died? Papers? A disk of any kind. A memory stick? Look. I know we've been through all this before...'

A thousand times or more.

'You told me you felt stricken with guilt because you weren't there when he needed you. That you were in Brussels on some government thing. With a man...a lobbyist...who was called...Mark...O'Malley, or was it?' He rubbed his chin. He glanced down at a notebook and then he looked up. 'It wasn't O'Malley. It was Mark Money.'

And in that moment I knew.

I stopped his hand, took the cigarette from his fingers, placed it in my own mouth, sucking in the bitter truth of this man, and said, my eyes hardening, 'How do you know about him? I told you about the business trip, but I never mentioned any name. What do you take me for?'

And all the time I'd zoned out, been so in my own head, someone, maybe it was Stevie, had somehow put Ray's silver gun in my hand.

Ray looked ashen, dead already, slightly surprised.

I sat back and thought about ligature marks, the so-called suicide, and how Stevie would never have done that, sullied his sacred river. I put my finger on the trigger and said, 'I'll give you the memory stick. I know where it is. But first of all let's talk a little bit more about Mark Money, what you know about him, if he sent you here, and also about what really happened to Stevie ...'

Outside, dawn is breaking. Copper streaks on the surface of the Thames. But inside the boat, the air is thick and gloomy as we talk about money, death, love and life and how both of us are liars and how Stevie was too good for either of us, how neither of us deserved him in the end.

And maybe we could work things out, get over ourselves, our corrupted lives, do some sort of deal – who knows? Find a glimmer of hope in all this darkness. But, you see, things have a way of working out much quicker than that when you're deranged with grief, mad with love, love you can no longer have, and you know you've been betrayed and have debts to pay to a man who went by the name of Mark Money, and, most of all, you have a gun in your hand.

CHANCE

LAURA WILSON

'I was fortunate to learn my craft in rep. It was a real apprenticeship, the best sort of training, one that actors today simply don't get. Very hard work, but lots of fun at the same time, and being part of an ensemble, with everyone absolutely supporting each other, doing all sorts of different things – Shakespeare, modern classics, Agatha Christie, pantomime... There was that feeling of a living skill, that one was connected somehow, all the way back to Burbage, to those bands of travelling players – and you had the opportunity to work with all these wonderful older actors, so of course you learned from them without realising you were learning, so that was marvellous, and you'd get these terrific old characters working in the regional theatres, managers and flymen and so on...

'Oh, yes, Philip Porter. I was lucky enough to work with him in the mid-seventies. That was the last play he did, and, of course, he died. That was so sad, and awful, really, because it happened right onstage. He hadn't been well, but it was quite a shock. He was a lovely man, a true star and a great loss to the profession.

'The play was called *How's Your Father?* Roger Flemyng was in it too – that was before he was transported to the heights in Hollywood, but you could tell he was going to be a star, and, of course, he was terrifically handsome...It was Philip who was the name, though: all those comedy films, the TV series, and he'd had a single in the Top Ten as well, with an old Cockney song called "I'm Henery the Eighth, I Am"...

'Anyway. The plot was about a widower whose son and daughter are terribly strait-laced and convinced he's having it off with lots of women and it's going to affect their standing in the community, and then they decide he's carrying on with a man as well. It's the sort of thing that never gets put on now because of the sexism and homophobia, but it was harmless really. There was a lot of what's called stage business – you know, with props and so forth, and people jumping in and out of cupboards and all the rest of it. I remember I spent most of it running around wearing not very much. I always had a coat in the wings because it was winter and we were touring in the north, and some of the theatres – lovely old places, real works of art, but most of them gone now, I think, which is a shame – could get pretty nippy. We were all so sorry about Philip. They did get someone to replace him in the part, but it wasn't the same, because we'd had such fun doing it. Really tremendous camaraderie, playing jokes on each other and that sort of thing.

'After that ended, I was up for a part in *Crossroads* – I'd had a cough and a spit in the series about six months earlier, and they wanted me back, but of course, you're never sure if these things are going to happen, so I got another job...'

This was the point at which the factual material of Denise's acting career ran out (unless you counted a three-month trudge round old people's homes playing Cinderella), so that continuing the imaginary interview was harder work. Up to there it was, however, true, except that she'd never actually done any Shakespeare, and it was probably stretching it a bit to describe *Night Must Fall* and *Arsenic and Old Lace* as actual modern classics, although she could claim parts – small ones, but nevertheless – in *You Never Can Tell* and *An Inspector Calls.*

The problem was that Denise had never quite been able to settle on a definitive narrative for what she thought of as the first option for her projected career: constant work, yes; important, even groundbreaking parts, yes; acclaim and awards, yes; national-treasure status now, at sixty-five, yes; a persona gracious yet fun-loving, spirited and, above all, grounded, yes – but the specifics varied and had to be thought out afresh each time. Sitting on a plastic chair in the busy corridor of a London hospital and waiting for a mammogram wasn't really conducive to comparing and contrasting the merits of an internationally lauded TV series versus a respected and long-running film franchise, or the Royal Shakespeare Company versus the National Theatre, or a BAFTA versus a Golden Globe. She'd never considered giving herself all of them – that would have been not only greedy, but untenably deluded.

Now, here, at eleven fifteen on a November morning, she went with the second option – talking about how the death of Philip Porter had jinxed her career. This she did as the author of a universally acclaimed, sell-out play based on her experience, which she knew she would write one day. She had actually made some notes, but, thus far, she hadn't managed to get any further. The problem was that she could never quite see how the play would end. Obviously something very dramatic would need to happen, but what?

Despite this, the second option was, on the whole, easier, because it was based on truth; Philip's jealous wife, Maggie, had seen to that. The device of it being the basis for a play was necessary, partly because if Denise was going to write it and it be performed in the West End, she might as well get into practice answering questions about it, and also because the sheer spiteful *cruelty* of what Maggie Porter had done in robbing her of a career was only bearable if considered at one remove.

Denise had never confronted Maggie about the snide comments, the slow, steady drips of poison and the insidious use of her influence as Philip's widow to prevent her getting the part in *Crossroads* or any of the other jobs. It had, in fact, been several years before she'd actually realised what was going on – after all, anyone could have a run of bad luck – and quite a lot more years, hoping against hope, before she understood the extent of the devastation. By then it was too late: her time had passed, her agent had given up on her, and her contacts, such as they were, had dwindled to nothing. She'd put a brave face on it, pretending she hadn't been ambitious and didn't really care, never telling anyone about Maggie for fear of driving her friends away with her bitterness and thwarted ambition. Someone had mentioned, in passing, that Maggie had gone to live in Australia, but it was difficult to find people in those days because the technology wasn't there. It was too late now anyway, because Maggie, when finally tracked down via the Internet, turned out to have died in 2004.

Still, at least Denise didn't really have to worry about the results of the mammogram. Hospitals made you feel uncomfortable, certainly – the unseen bedridden congregations in the wards above one's head constant reminders of what would happen, not now, not yet, but sometime ... But there was no family history of cancer, and she had a healthy lifestyle – after giving up, or rather being given up by, the stage, Denise had become first an aromatherapist and then a yoga teacher, and she practised what she preached. 'I'm lucky,' she told her fictional interlocutor now, 'I can still fit into clothes I bought forty years ago, although obviously –' she gave a playful laugh '– I have to do a bit more, let's say –' with a roll of the eyes '– *strategic draping* with scarves and things.'

In any case, her time wasn't now. She knew that. Her lifeline was long and deep – plenty of vitality – and her star chart indicated a long life too. It also confirmed that she was destined to work in the arts – a Leo with a full fifth house, which meant that she was a free spirit, a risk-taker, a creative person with no fear of spontaneous self-expression, pleasure or love. The fifth house governed children (another form of creativity) too, but she'd concentrated for so long on trying to breathe life into her flagging career that she'd passed up such opportunities as had materialised. Maggie Porter's act of misplaced revenge was responsible for that as well.

If only she'd been able to explain to the woman that Philip's death had had nothing to do with her. 'Which she must have known,' Denise now told the imaginary interviewer. 'After all, it was a pretty strenuous part and he wasn't in particularly good health, although he was only in his sixties...' *The same age I am now,* she thought, remembering how Philip would nap in the cluttered, shabby dressing room, his seamed face slack in repose, and how, standing near him onstage, she'd hear him wheezing. 'His reputation as a womaniser was hardly a secret. Maggie was always there, in the theatre, and that was partly keeping an eye on him, not just the worry about his physical condition. Obviously grief makes people irrational, so I think she made me a scapegoat, really.' Except – should she actually say that? She'd been over and over this in her head, but the fact was that it would be very hard to explain the play without mentioning Maggie standing there night after night in the wings, watching with baleful eyes as she and Terri Fanshaw, both playing the 'totty' roles, dashed on and off the stage in their underwear.

She didn't want people to think she was vindictive or point-scoring, especially as Maggie was no longer around to put her side of the story. What she needed to convey was that she'd managed to overcome – transcend, even – her feelings of anger, frustration and disappointment, thereby gaining maturity and insight. 'Writing, one learns to objectify experience,' she told the journalist (it would be the review pages of the *Guardian* on Saturday, perhaps, or the *Sunday Times*). 'You stand outside your life so that it's not about you any more, but something altogether bigger. I suppose from Maggie's point of view, the thing was that I was the one onstage with Philip when it happened. I gave him the cue – there was a running gag about a brown wig that kept getting moved about and mistaken for a rat and so on, and I had to say, "Did you get rid of it?" When he didn't answer, I thought he was messing about, because, as I say, we'd all been playing tricks on each other. There was a tray of cocktails that got passed round and people put pepper and things in the glasses, and there was one scene where Philip's character had to tear up a bunch of envelopes and someone put bits of balsa wood inside them, that sort of thing... So I started ad-libbing and then I realised that something was wrong. I came off and got them to bring the curtain down. The audience were laughing – they thought it was part of the play, even when we asked if there was a doctor in the house – and I don't think he thought it was real either until he actually had a look at Philip. Maggie was standing there watching all this, and she got the idea that it was my fault. She told the others that I'd been messing about with the cocktail I'd given Philip – that was just before I said the line – and that the taste had given him a shock that caused the heart attack, but I hadn't, and –'

'Denise Dixon, as I live and breathe.'

Denise's eyes flew open. In front of her was a man in a wheelchair, shrunken by age and overlarge pyjamas and robe, with rheumy eyes, parchment skin cling-filmed across the planes of an almost hairless skull, and a cannula attached to one skeletal, liver-spotted hand. 'Mind you,' he said, 'I'm barely doing either.'

'Either of what?'

'Living or breathing. You don't remember me, do you?'

'I'm sorry, I ...'

'That smutty thing we were in together. When Philip Porter died.'

Denise leaned forward. 'Leslie Boxer! Of course, you and Angela...' She pictured Angela Warner – in her late thirties then, petite, all impish (or, to Denise's way of thinking, chipmunky) prettiness and mischievous charm. Now she looked past Leslie and down the corridor. 'Is she here?'

Leslie shook his head. 'We parted company some years ago. Last seen playing a corpse in *Casualty*. What was the name of that bloody play anyway? *Get Your Cock Out?*'

'*How's Your Father?*'

'Yes, of course it was.' He said this in a way that made her think he'd known the title all along. 'God, the shit one did in those days.'

A gob of spittle flew out of his mouth and landed on a fold of Denise's scarf, where it clung momentarily, like a tiny brooch. Leslie had always, she now remembered, been pawkily matter-of-fact in person, which was entirely at odds with the chillily distinguished, silky-voiced types – High

Court judges, members of the House of Lords – that he'd played for much of his career. Crestfallen and stung by his vehemence, she protested, 'It wasn't all that bad.'

'It *was*. Trudging round those freezing dumps, playing that rubbish. Digs in dreary terraces, sets so flimsy they might have been made out of cornflake packets. Besides which – and it rains all the bloody time in those northern towns – if you ever managed a walk without being drenched, all you'd see was corrugated iron and canals full of shopping trolleys. Everything filthy... and that fucking terrible play!'

His voice, once rich and smooth, was now tremulous and reedy, and he spoke in bursts, pausing to snatch at breath. 'I admit the play wasn't up to much,' said Denise, 'but some of those theatres were *lovely*.'

'In 1900 maybe, but –' he shook his head '– I remember one place on that tour where the sofa kept rolling off the set by itself and you had to hang on to the bloody thing while you were saying your lines. And one where the stage manager was pissed the entire time. And one where the ASM was as deaf as a post and kept cueing everything at the wrong moments.'

'I know, but they had the most wonderful histories! One of them had a ghost, didn't it? I thought I saw it once – in the stalls when no one was supposed to be there.'

'If it was a ghost, it probably came to warn poor old Philip. Except that it wasn't. What you saw was a caretaker or a cleaner, if you really saw anything at all. The human mind's like that. We can convince ourselves of anything – turn black into white and vice versa. You just hadn't done enough touring for the excitement to wear off, dear. Don't you remember? We were all so bored we were playing jokes on each other because it was the only way to get through the thing.' He paused, staring at her intently. 'Are you waiting for someone, or what?'

'Just a mammogram. The waiting room's full and they parked me out here, so I think it could take some time.'

'At least you'll be leaving. I won't.'

'I'm sorry. Is it...?'

'Cancer? Yes. A lot of it.'

'I'm sorry.'

'It's not your fault.' He shrugged. 'Something's got to take you off, and I'm nearly ninety.'

'All the same...'

He shook his head. 'I doubt I'll be able to sit here chatting to you like this by next week, but there it is. No use crying over spilt milk. Don't suppose you'd mind either if you were my age. Where have you been all this time, anyway?' He put his head on one side and stared at her beadily. 'You didn't do a lot after that play, did you?'

'Not much, no. But I see *you* on television all the time. Theatre too.'

He wasn't going to be deflected. 'I've done OK. Marriage and kids, was it?'

Denise shook her head, unsure of what to say, then realised that she'd waited a beat too long to make light of her failure to continue in the profession. Looking at Leslie, who stared back with watery impassivity, she felt the urge to confide. He had been there, after all, so he'd understand about Maggie, and he was dying, so there was little chance of his making her seem pitiful by telling people. It would be an unburdening, almost like a confession – although, of course, those were supposed to be for your own sins, not other people's, although presumably other people's came into it as well, quite often... And Leslie had played a few clergymen in his time, hadn't he? Although not religious,

Denise was a deeply spiritual person, and perhaps...Here, like a shipwreck brought groaning to the surface, the claggy emotional mass of damage done rose up inside her, so that she felt her eyes well with tears.

Leslie exhaled a long, rattling sigh. 'Do you want to tell me?'

'It was Maggie.'

'Maggie?'

'Maggie Porter.'

'Philip's wife?' Leslie looked puzzled. 'I liked her. Always brought packets of Jacob's Club biscuits in and shared them round. And those chocolate bars they don't make any more...Golden Cup, I think they were called. Toffee in the middle. Very nice.'

Denise blinked. 'Did she? You've got a good memory.'

'But not for the things that matter, it seems. What did Maggie do to you?'

'Destroyed my career. She thought I'd put something in Philip's drink.'

'But Philip had a heart attack.'

'I know, but she thought I'd caused it – given him a shock or something. I know we'd all been messing about, but it was nothing to do with me. I sometimes wonder if she hadn't got it into her head that he was in love with me or something. I mean, he'd made a pass at me, but that was...you know...'

'A reflex action,' said Leslie. 'Like blowing his nose.'

'I know,' said Denise, slightly nettled. 'But all the same...'

'Maggie would have known that was all it was, dear. They'd been married for nearly twenty years, so she'd seen it often enough. Did she accuse you of anything?'

'Not in so many words, but she told me it was my fault. She said I'd messed about with the drink and then just stood there simpering while Philip...while he...' Denise closed her eyes in an effort to stop the tears coming, remembering

Maggie's furious face inches from her own, a fleck of lipstick on her bared teeth, her absolute, implacable fury.

'That was shock, dear. Takes people in different ways.'

'Yes, but she *blamed* me.'

'Only for not reacting more quickly. She would have said those things to anyone – me, Angela, Roger Flemyng, any one of us – if we'd been onstage with him.'

'It was more than that. After all, *she* could have done something; she was there too. In the wings, watching. She was always bloody there.'

'No, she wasn't.'

'Yes, she was, she –'

'No. Not when Philip died.'

'She was. I saw her when I went on. I remember it because I had to make the entrance running – she was in the way and I dodged past her and practically fell on to the stage. It got a laugh, so Philip had to wait before he said his line. I remember it clearly.'

'At that point, perhaps, but you'd had a few pages of dialogue before it happened, hadn't you?'

'Yes, a load of stuff about the prospective buyers coming to look at the house and seeing the rat and the wife having hysterics. But she was *there*, Leslie. I know she was.'

Leslie shook his head. 'Not when it happened. She was upstairs, talking to me. The ASM came and told us that Philip had been taken ill.'

'But then…' Denise stared at him, as thrown off balance as if she had stepped off a moving merry-go-round, 'Afterwards, why did she say those things?'

'What things?'

'To all her friends in the business – the producer at *Crossroads*, the plays I was up for. She knew everyone, Leslie, because of Philip, and she told them all.'

'Told them all what?'

'That it was my fault. Oh, I'm sure she didn't actually accuse me of murder or anything, but she'll have hinted that I was responsible – that I was jinxed, unlucky. You *know* how superstitious people are in the profession, Leslie. Anything with a whiff of disaster or failure or anything like that, they don't want to be associated with it in case they're contaminated somehow. My agent stopped returning my calls, and I started noticing that people were – well, not exactly avoiding me, but they weren't so friendly any more, and... Well, it was as if they just wanted me to disappear or something. I couldn't get auditions, let alone callbacks. I'd been doing well until that happened, and then it all just ground to a halt.'

Leslie's gaze was both pitying and somehow remote; neutral sympathy, as of a doctor or priest.

'Do you see what I'm saying?' she asked. 'Maggie made that happen.'

'No.' Leslie raised a quivering hand to stop Denise contradicting him. 'That's what I was talking about when I said we're able to convince ourselves of anything. Acting's a brutal profession – all the rejection and disappointment – and the effort of keeping yourself intact in the face of that when success is the only thing that matters, that's tough, and a lot of people can't handle it. So you start to believe – even more than people in other walks of life – that you got a part or made something good happen because you're so talented or beautiful or whatever it is, but when you fail, that's down to bad luck or someone shafting you.'

'She *did* shaft me.'

Leslie sighed again, an even harsher sound this time, and closed his eyes. When he opened them, he seemed to be peering at her from a long way away, as though she had dwindled to a dot on a horizon. 'What happened to Philip was a tragedy, but nobody blamed you, because there was no reason to. Maggie might have said a few things to a few people because she was angry and upset, but it wouldn't have made any difference because she simply didn't have that much influence, dear. Yes, she was Philip's widow, and everybody liked her – and felt pretty sorry for her, because of the way he carried on – but that was as far as it went.'

Denise's entire body felt as cold and rigid as if it had been filled with cement, so that, for a moment, she was unable to move or speak. 'But...' Her voice broke on the word.

'It's the business, dear, that's all. It's...' Leslie paused. 'I was going to say "unfair", but I think "indifferent" is probably more accurate. I mean, when I started, I was sure I was going to play Hamlet, but the leading roles never materialised. Philip didn't deserve to die like he did, in a piece of crap, miles away from home, with everybody laughing at him because they thought he was hamming it up and then talking a lot of bollocks afterwards about how it was "what he would have wanted", as if any of them had a clue... And look at Roger Flemyng...' Leslie's words were coming in gasps now, and they were like projectiles hurled at her so that she drew back, blinking, at the onslaught. 'That shit got... fucking... *everything*... and the only thing he could do was wear a fucking cravat. That TV series – the spy thing – he got that straight after, and then all those films – Hollywood – lounging by his fucking pool and telling everyone how he'd come up the hard way... Talentless *cunt*.'

The last word broke over her in a shower of phlegmy spray and was followed by a prolonged fit of coughing so violent that it seemed almost to tear him in two.

'Leslie!' Denise leaned forward and put a hand on his knee. 'Shall I fetch someone?'

He flapped a tremulous hand at her. 'No ... *Christ* ... Fine ... Give me a minute.'

The racking and heaving gradually subsided. Leslie fumbled in his capacious robe for an agonisingly long time before producing a tissue and wiping his mouth with it. 'Sorry, dear.'

'I had no idea you hated him so much.'

'You had no idea what was going on, dear.' Leslie paused to cough again. 'You wouldn't have come out with all that stuff about Maggie if you had.'

Denise felt as precarious as if she were walking a high wire with Leslie a long way below, his face just a chalky blur. Carefully, and with great attention, she said, 'What do you mean, exactly?'

Leslie closed one eye and grimaced in the manner of a man about to manoeuvre a grand piano through a narrow doorway. Then, leaning forward with a visible effort, he fixed both his eyes on hers and said, 'I suppose I might as well tell you. I've never told anyone before, but it can't make any difference now that I'm almost a corpse. I didn't want to do that bloody play, but God knows there wasn't anything else at the time. That limp-wristed estate agent wasn't in the usual run of things I got offered, and it wasn't much of a part, but all I'd had in twelve months were a couple of films – a puerile sex farce, and one of those preposterous Hammer things where I flapped about in a black cloak and sacrificed virgins. Angela said it would be nice to do something where we could work together for once, so I agreed. What I didn't know was that she wanted to do it because of Roger. She'd been seeing him behind my back for a few months, and she was obsessed by him. I loved her so much, Denise. More than I've ever loved anyone. When I realised what was going on – it was a couple of weeks in,

I suppose, before the penny really dropped – I was devastated. Couldn't eat, couldn't sleep – all I could do was think about the two of them together.

'Maggie knew. She spotted it – years of practice being married to Philip, I suppose. She told me to let it run its course, that Angela would realise which side her bread was buttered and come back to me, but I was sure she wouldn't. Angela wasn't a compulsive adulterer like Philip. The thing she had with Roger wasn't just opportunistic self-gratification, because that wasn't how she was. She was – or believed she was – utterly in love with Roger, and it wasn't just that I didn't want to lose her; I didn't want that prancing, smirking *tit* to have her either. He was so barefaced about it – utterly shameless, as if it were his right... At one point – we were in Oldham and all the bigwigs were in – he was actually "off" because he was fucking *my* wife in the dressing room, and there *I* was extemporising in front of the Chamber of fucking Commerce.

'All I could think about was that if I got him out of the way, Angela would come back to me. I managed to get hold of some tincture of aconite. In large doses, 50 ml or more, it works pretty fast and it's fatal. Roger's character made an entrance in the second act about six pages after you did, and the stage direction was for him to take one of the cocktails off the tray and knock it back in one gulp. There was all that plot stuff about rat poison – that wig they thought was a rodent – and thinking it had got into the cocktails, and trying to grab glasses off people before they could drink and whatnot... Do you remember?'

Denise nodded. 'The tray was on the coffee table, wasn't it?'

'Yes. A round one. The ASM was supposed to set it during the interval, but she was in a flap because there was something wrong with the curtain, so I said I'd get the stuff on to the stage while she sorted it out. I doctored one glass and positioned it very carefully so that Roger would be sure to pick up that particular one – but you must have nudged the tray round, so Philip got it.'

'No... no...' Denise closed her eyes and shook her head.

'You were the only one onstage, apart from Philip, and he was just sitting on the sofa, remember? That was the blocking – you were tidying up around him.'

'I didn't touch the tray.' Had she touched it? She couldn't remember. Apart from nearly falling on to the stage because of Maggie, everything was a blank up until the point when she'd realised that Philip wasn't responding.

'Philip's character had a drink, remember? It was that glass.'

'How do you know? They were all the same.'

'I looked afterwards. I'd deliberately scattered a few crumbs from one of Maggie's Jacob's Club biscuits around the base of the glass so I'd be sure to position the tray correctly, and that was the one that got moved. No one would blame you if you'd switched the tray round, Denise. Everyone was messing about, remember – and even if you weren't, that sort of thing is easily done when you've got business and dialogue at the same time.'

'So... you're saying *I* killed Philip?'

'No, dear, I'm saying it was an accident. That heart attack could have happened at any time. Philip was a heavy drinker, he smoked like a chimney and he had a dicky ticker. Maggie said the doctor kept telling him to give up – the fags and the booze – but he wouldn't take any notice. Philip might have had months, perhaps as much as a year, without the aconite, but it would have happened sooner or later, and Maggie knew it. I felt terrible that I'd robbed her of that extra time with him, and of course, it didn't do me any good either – Roger went shooting off into the stratosphere, and Angela left me two years later for somebody else.'

'But... So...'

'So it was nothing to do with you at all.'

Blood jackhammered in Denise's ears as the edifice of her life, carefully constructed over four decades, crashed down around her. 'So,' she said finally, 'what I told you – Maggie, the jinx, the ... *blight* – it was all a delusion?'

'I'm afraid so, dear. Shit happens. Or, if you're religious, try "Man makes plans, and God laughs" if it makes you feel better.'

'But I was meant –' At this point, Denise's name was called out by a harassed-looking nurse who'd appeared with a clipboard. She rose, unsteadily. 'This won't take very long ... Will you be here when I get back?'

'No, dear. I've said all I needed to. Rather glad I bumped into you, actually.'

'So that's all?' she said stupidly. 'That's it?'

Leslie nodded. 'You'll be all right.' Raising his cannulated hand in a sketchy salute, he added, 'And I shouldn't feel too badly about the career. After all, dear, you were hardly Judi Dench, were you?'

The nurse, impatient now, summoned her once more, and Denise turned to follow her through the waiting room to the cubicle where she would sit, naked from the waist up, until she was summoned before the machine.

Natural Justice

Kate Rhodes

O n the night of his retirement party, crows gathered on the roof of Robert Cregan's house. They perched on the ridge pole, silent as black-coated old men attending a funeral, attracted by raised voices drifting from an upstairs window. Inside the master bedroom Cregan was conducting a shouting match with his wife.

'Get ready, Lou. We're leaving in ten minutes.'

'I told you I'm staying here.' She stared at the carpet when she spoke.

It crossed Cregan's mind to give her a slap to bring her round, but that always left a bad aftertaste; her behaviour couldn't be allowed to taint his evening. Instead he turned away and marched downstairs.

Rain pelted the ground as he waited on the porch, splattering mud across his best shoes. Once the taxi's headlights rounded the corner, he rushed down the path, but something struck him hard on the shoulder before he reached the gate. His fists curled in self-defence as a bird flapped past his face, wings outstretched, its raucous cry ringing in his ears. Cregan lashed out, knuckles pounding against the softness of feathers. The crow landed on the path, pert head twisted at an angle, a long tear through one of its wings.

Anger boiled inside Cregan's chest – there was something disgusting about the way those coal-black feathers glistened in the street light. He brought his foot down hard, the bird's skull shattering under his heel with a satisfying crunch.

He forgot about the creature once the cab pulled away. The twenty-minute journey gave Cregan time for nostalgia. He had enjoyed a long career in the Metropolitan Police, spending years on the beat, rising eventually to the rank of custody sergeant. It had been his job to deal with every mis- creant and petty thief that arrived at the station. His hair might have thinned since he joined the force, and his waist- line now strained the buttons of his suit, but his confidence was undimmed. Only his wife's disloyalty bothered him. She should be at his side through tonight's speeches and tributes. It was her body language that had annoyed him most, arms folded, her mouth set in a grim line. Louise's attitude was a problem he would have to deal with once and for all when he got home.

It was a relief to hear laughter spilling from the doors of the police social club. The food was bound to be shit, and so was the wine, but at least both would be plentiful. Police parties weren't for the faint-hearted. By ten o'clock he was drunk enough not to care who toasted his glorious career; once he'd made his farewell speech, he could relax. Only the old lags stayed past midnight, soaking up free booze like litmus paper. He had a vague memory of singing 'My Way' at the top of his voice and pulling the blondest bar- maid on to his lap for a quick squeeze before the bounc- ers chucked him out. Cregan's boss caught up with him as the rest of the party vanished into the night. The DI was a decade younger than him, fitter too, with a university edu- cation, but they'd always rubbed along. He braced himself for more good wishes, but none arrived.

'I need a word, Rob, before you leave,' the younger man said. 'I'm afraid there's going to be another enquiry.'

Cregan stared at him. 'I'm no longer a serving officer.'

'That doesn't help; the relatives are kicking up a fuss.'

'What do you mean?'

'They're talking about legal action. We'll argue self-defence, of course. Sorry to leave it till now; I didn't want to spoil your evening.'

Cregan found himself alone on the pavement, head spinning with tinny music, brandy and bad news. The first inquiry should have solved the problem. Six months ago some drug-dealing scumbag had lost it in a holding cell. How was he to know that the swift kick he'd delivered to shut him up would rupture the man's spleen? He had been found dead the next morning. Internal bleeding. Luckily another officer had been standing behind him, obscuring the CCTV, but the bloke's brother had refused to shut up. He flagged down another taxi home, reassuring himself that one misjudgement was nothing in the context of a twenty-eight-year career. Counting the names of the villains he'd arrested for burglary, rape, and murder had rocked him to sleep at night. Natural justice had been his watch-word: an eye for an eye, a tooth for a tooth; nothing went unpunished. He was still glowing with remembered pride when he staggered back up to his front door.

He called his wife's name, but his voice echoed in the hallway. She was probably cowering under the covers, scared of recriminations. His jaw clenched as he stumbled up the stairs. The bed had been made, but Louise was nowhere to be seen. He punched the wall twice, then let out a string of expletives as his knuckles burned. He took three more steps then toppled face first on to the pristine bed, unconscious before he'd closed his eyes.

Cregan woke with a force-ten hangover. His head felt like someone had tried to cleave it from his shoulders. He stumbled around the house, ignoring the pain stabbing behind his eyes. Even in his weakened state he saw that things were missing: the brand-new coffee machine, pictures from the living-room wall, an antique chair. Louise must have been planning it for months. While his farewell party was in full swing, some creep had helped her load a van and drive it away.

He rang his wife's mobile but got no reply. Her sister pleaded ignorance, and the manager of the hairdresser's where she worked pretended to be shocked. The woman's smug voice made him hurl his phone at the wall. Louise would crawl home soon enough, and when she did, he'd make her eat a ton of humble pie. In the meantime he would enjoy himself. No one could stop him smoking indoors, swilling beer from the can, shagging whoever he chose.

Cregan cooked himself a full English, the breakfast Louise never allowed. It was only when he'd finished eating that he noticed an unusual sound. A raw shriek that wouldn't let up. When he opened the back door, the source was obvious. Birds hovered at the bottom of the garden, black flakes of soot circling overhead. Why hadn't he heard them before? Maybe they only called during the day when he'd been at work. Their cry was faint but grating, a cross between a child's scream and fingernails scraping across a blackboard.

He went back indoors to recruit mates for a pub crawl. What he needed was an afternoon of anecdotes, beer and wisecracks. He flicked on his mobile and placed another call.

'How's retirement treating you, Smithy?' he asked.

'Not bad, old son. Sorry to miss your shindig.'

Smithy talked about his wife's illness, banging on about dialysis and transplant lists. The poor sod couldn't leave her alone for five minutes. Cregan flicked through the numbers on his phone, but all of his friends had reasons not to come – prior engagements or laying off the booze. He considered driving to the golf club, but the blokes there bored him rigid. His brother would have joined him, but he lived two hundred miles away.

At five o'clock he left another message on Louise's phone, doing his best to sound calm. He told her to stop playing silly buggers and come home. The fact that she didn't pick up made him angry enough to grab his keys and rush outside. That was when he saw the crow's body splayed across the path. Something had feasted on it overnight, guts smeared across the cobblestones, eye sockets picked clean. Cregan's stomach churned. He couldn't face scraping the creature's remains into a bin bag, so he stepped over it to unlock the car without looking down.

The Red Lion had changed since his last visit. It used to be a coppers' pub, old boys lining up pints on the bar, but now everyone looked underage. All the girls were beddable, but most had a boyfriend in tow. None of them cast a glance in his direction. Music pulsed from speakers above the bar, scratchy and disjointed, the volume too high to hear himself think. He kept his coat on while he downed his beer. There were no messages on his phone, except one from his mother, rambling about nothing in particular. It was a relief to get back outside, rain battering his face as he sprinted to the car.

Cregan spent the next three days holed up indoors, eating takeaway food and knocking back booze. When sleep deserted him, he watched late-night films that ended with explosions and car chases, but when the screen finally blanked, the crows' cawing was too raucous to ignore. They circled the house for hours, their cries piercing the thin glass of his bedroom window.

The next morning he received a phone call, a solicitor's cool voice inviting him to her office for mediation. She informed him that Louise hoped a settlement could be agreed upon before she applied for a divorce. Cregan listened in stunned silence; the lawyer explained that mediation would allow their assets to be divided fairly and save them a fortune in legal fees.

'Like hell it will. I'll take her to the cleaners; she won't get a penny.'

'Then we'll see you in court, Mr Cregan.' She hung up with a crisp goodbye. When the call finished, the crows' screams were louder than ever.

By the end of the week Cregan phoned a pest-control company. The manager sounded incredulous when he explained the problem.

'We can't help with crows, sir, just rats, mice and foxes. Birds, we don't touch.'

'Who does?'

'No one, far as I know. You could try mixing rat poison with breadcrumbs.'

Cregan followed the man's instructions, scattering handfuls of the mixture on the lawn. The crows circled high overhead, considering the nature of his gift. But the next afternoon it was clear his plan had backfired. Two blackbirds and a robin lay dead on the grass, thin legs stretched stiffly away from their bodies. At first he thought that the crows had disappeared, until they erupted into the sky, tainting the air with blackness, their shrieks louder than playground insults. They flew so close that their odour of dust and decaying meat stuck in Cregan's throat. He grabbed at them, but they danced above his head, impossible to reach. Now he shook the entire box of poison on to the lawn, small grey nuggets littering the grass. Afterwards he stared up at the crows' nests with gritted teeth, determined to gain the upper hand. If necessary, he would pay someone to cut the tree down.

That night the crows' calls were deafening. They drowned out the TV, no matter how high he pumped the volume. He needed earplugs to snatch a few hours' sleep, the noise forcing him to bury his head under the pillow. Cregan's insomnia put him off his food, a hot pain searing the roof of his skull. Unable to face breakfast, he donned his wellingtons and went outside. Rage hit him as he walked down the path. The lawn had become an avian graveyard. The corpses of blue tits, chaffinches, and pigeons were strewn at his feet, glassy eyes fixed on the November sky. Not one crow had succumbed to his poison.

Cregan was about to go back inside to call a tree surgeon when his vision blurred. Suddenly the pain grew unbearable, thoughts slowing to a standstill. He fell forward, face twisted painfully to one side. It was impossible to move; even lifting his fingers demanded too much effort. He was still trying to gather his strength when something rustled in the grass nearby. A crow's black face appeared inches from his own. Its eyes were clear gold, feathers gleaming like anthracite, beak shiny as wet slate. His head swam with emotions he couldn't identify. Up close the creature was far more beautiful than he'd realised. But he didn't have long to admire it. He was too weak to blink when the crows dived at him, too many to count. His last vision was of the flock itself. A murder of them, escaping into the sky, then plunging down to attack him again.

MEET THE KILLER WOMEN

Killer Women is a group of London-based crime writers who collaborate to produce innovative events, publications, debates and workshops. You can find a complete list of associated writers at www.killerwomen.org.

Below, the contributors to this first Killer Women anthology introduce themselves and their work.

JANE CASEY

What kind of books do you write?
I write a series of police procedural novels featuring a London-Irish detective sergeant in a Metropolitan Police murder investigation team, Maeve Kerrigan. I've also written psychological thrillers and a crime series for teenagers. Everything I write turns to crime!

What did you do before you became a writer?
I was a children's books editor, specialising in teen fiction. I loved my job, but I used to get up two hours early to write the book that turned into my first novel, *The Missing*. Children's fiction is a specialised part of publishing and it didn't directly help me to find an agent or get a book deal, but it was a great job. I still miss the thrill of acquiring a great manuscript.

What are you proudest of?

I won Crime Novel of the Year award at the Irish Book Awards in 2015, for *After the Fire*. It was my fifth time to be nominated and I was used to losing! I was also thrilled to win the Mary Higgins Clark Award in the US for *The Stranger You Know*. Mary Higgins Clark is a great writer and an icon in US crime fiction, so getting her seal of approval was hugely encouraging.

What was your inspiration for the story in this collection?

I used to live in a flat like the one in 'The Rat Trap' except it was on the ground floor. I found it claustrophobic to be living so close to so many neighbours, yet I didn't really know what was going on in their lives – Londoners tend to keep themselves to themselves, and the closer they live to one another, the more distant they seem to be. All crime writers are obsessed with what goes on behind closed doors: in this case, what goes on is particularly dark…

TAMMY COHEN

What kind of books do you write?

I started off writing dark contemporary women's fiction and now write dark psychological thrillers. Apparently.

What did you do before you became a writer?

Do you 'become' a writer? I think probably you either are one or you're not. As a kid I used to make little homemade books tied with string to give to my long-suffering parents, and even when I was teaching English in Spain or being the World's Worst Secretary, I was always writing on the side, just not earning money from it. Then came journalism, which is a very different type of writing, followed by non-fiction, and when I finally got my first novel published at the age of forty-seven, after having been a 'writer' in my head for nearly half a century, there was just this relieved sense of 'at last'.

What are you proudest of?
Julie Burchill messaging me to say how much she'd loved *The Broken* was huge for me, as she was such an iconic figure in my teens and twenties. Also, my twenty-one-year-old son reading *When She Was Bad* recently – the first of my three kids to read any of my books – and pronouncing it 'pretty good'.

What was your inspiration for your story in this collection?
We used to have a house in North London around the corner from 23d Cranley Gardens, where serial killer Dennis Nilson butchered and dismembered at least three of his victims. Every time I'd walk past his old flat, I'd imagine what it would be like to live there now, with all those ghosts, and wonder whether the new owners had chosen it in spite of its history or because of it, and what that might say about them.

SARAH HILARY

What kind of books do you write?
Police procedurals with a side order of psychological thriller.

What did you do before you became a writer?
Read books, worked with the Royal Navy, read more books.

What are you proudest of?
Winning the Theakston's Old Peculier Crime Novel of the Year for my debut, *Someone Else's Skin*.

What was your inspiration for your story in this collection?
A news snippet about a famous art collection destroyed by someone pulling the wrong plug from the wall. And the notion, always knocking about in my head, of lost children taken from their homes.

ERIN KELLY

What kind of books do you write?
Psychological thrillers that verge on the gothic. I'm interested in the way none of us can escape our pasts.

What did you do before you became a writer?
I was a feature writer for newspapers and magazines.

What are you proudest of?
Stephen King said of my novel *The Poison Tree*, 'I wish I'd written it.' That was a good moment, although the email came on April Fool's Day and I didn't believe it at first.

What was your inspiration for your story in this collection?
A Cath Kidston shop in which I nearly died of acute tweeness poisoning.

If you weren't a writer, what would you be?
In advertising, and much richer.

ALISON JOSEPH

What kind of books do you write?
I write contemporary detective fiction featuring Sister Agnes and DI Berenice Killick, and also a homeless Irishman called Malone, who's just appeared in his first short story

but is due to appear in a full-length novel called *Malone*. But then I was asked to write Agatha Christie as a detective, so for the first time in my writing life I'm also writing a series of novels set in the 1920s.

What did you do before you became a writer?
I worked in local radio, in Leeds, and then in television, making documentaries. I made a series for Channel 4 about women and religion, called *Through the Devil's Gateway*, presented by Helen Mirren. Soon after that it occurred to me to write a detective nun. The rest is history.

What are you proudest of?
If I'm proud of anything, it's the fact that I still sit down to my work each day with a sense of anticipation and enjoyment – a sense of 'what's going to happen next?' I have won awards such as one for best abridged radio production, for my work on *Captain Corelli's Mandolin* on BBC Radio 4, but awards are fleeting compared to the sense of still having a story to tell.

What was your inspiration for your story in this collection?
I wanted to write a crime story that had a simplicity about it, that allowed DI Berenice Killick to seem realistic as a copper. I wanted the characters to carry the story. I hope I've allowed them to do so.

ALEX MARWOOD

What kind of books do you write?
I think they're calling it 'psychological suspense' at the moment. It'll probably have another name next week.
What did you do before you became a writer?

Another sort of writer. And journalist (I mostly worked for *The Independent*, RIP) before that. Though I always secretly wanted to be a synchronised swimmer.

What are you proudest of?
The Edgar Award I won for *The Wicked Girls*. Oh, or having Stephen King call *The Killer Next Door* 'scary as hell'.

What was your inspiration for your story in this collection?
I absolutely adore the southwest of Malta and go there as often as I can. I was driving to Mdina from Birzebbugia one day and got lost, which happens often, as they have a rather whimsical way with road signs. After half an hour of driving down high-walled single-track roads before I finally emerged at the Neolithic temple at Hagar Qim, the story was pretty much fully formed in my head.

COLETTE MCBETH

What do you write?
Psychological thrillers, I suppose, but I think that's quite a wide church.

What did you do before you became an author?
I was a TV and political correspondent for BBC News. I still miss the thrill of live news.

If you weren't a writer, what would you be?
Where to start? I come up with something different every day. I love writing, but occasionally I get the feeling the practical part of my brain is underused. I'd love to develop my own business and I have an obsession with property and

renovating houses so maybe something that combined the two with a bit of TV thrown in.

What are you proudest of?
One of my favourite moments was opening up Twitter and seeing Marian Keyes raving about *The Life I Left Behind*. I'm a huge fan of hers – I basically want to be her – so that made all those days sitting in a lonely room doubting myself worthwhile.

What was your inspiration for the story in this collection?
Quite often it's an image that just pops into my head. So this time it was of a girl sitting high up on a roof, looking like she was going to jump.

M. J. MCGRATH

What kind of books do you write?
I write books with strong stories in several genres. Story is the thing for me.

What did you do before you became a writer?
I dreamed of becoming a writer.

What are you proudest of?
I've been lucky enough to make my living as a writer for twenty-four years.

What was your inspiration for your story in this collection?
In this story a young woman, unable to get over a failed relationship, finds her obsession slowly turning towards her elderly neighbour, whose lighthearted approach to romance drives the younger woman to a terrible act. In it

I wanted to explore the attitudes of two women at, respectively, the beginning and end of their romantic lives in a way that was both dark and humorous. The character of the elderly woman is inspired by a fabulous former neighbour of mine, a zesty nonagenarian with an admirable appetite for sixty-year-old toyboys.

KATE MEDINA

What kind of books do you write?
I write thrillers and crime novels with a strong psychological element. My debut novel, *White Crocodile*, is a thriller set in the minefields of northern Cambodia, which deals with the exploitation of women in both the developing and developed worlds. My second, *Fire Damage*, is the first in a series featuring psychologist Dr Jessie Flynn. *Fire Damage* is foremost a story about families: love and hate, kindness and cruelty, and the destructive nature of some relationships.

What did you do before you became a writer?
My parents have a photograph of me, aged seven, with a crew cut, wearing an army camouflage outfit. I was a very outdoorsy, wild child and always wanted to be a soldier, which is probably why I ended up spending five years in the Territorial Army and working for Jane's Information Group, the world's leading publisher of defence intelligence information.

I am lucky that I have a degree in psychology, which I think helps me enormously in developing complex characters who feel real. Because of my degree, I am also very drawn to people who have a different psychology from my own, whether that is in terms of mass cultural beliefs or individuals who, perhaps because of their upbringing or life experiences, display an abnormal psychology – all great fodder for a thriller writer!

What are you proudest of?
It is relatively early days for me as a thriller/crime writer, as I have only had two novels published so far, but to date I am proudest of *White Crocodile* being voted one of the Top Ten Crime Novels of the Year, 2016, by the American Library Association, which reviews over eight thousand books every year.

What was your inspiration for your story in this collection?
'Witch' is the fictionalised account of a real-life incident that occurred in Nigeria in 2016, in which a two-year-old boy, who had been cast out from his home because his family believed that he was a witch, was rescued from the streets by Anja Ringgren Loven, founder of African Children's Aid Education and Development Foundation, a charity that helps children who have been labelled as witches and thrown out of their communities.

D.E. MEREDITH

What kind of books do you write?
Historical forensic crime series set in the 1850s–60s, and now a contemporary crime series set in a mythical city.

What did you do before you became a writer?
Environmental and humanitarian campaigner

What are you proudest of?
I've never won anything, don't write bestsellers (shame!), but I love that my readers leave posts or email me or tweet me saying they want more.

What was your inspiration for your story in this collection?
The River Thames, a lost love, swans.

If I didn't write historical crime, I would write...
Short stories, flash fiction – I love the pithy, immediate form. I'd like to write them whilst flying in a biplane over the Hindu Kush or an endless African forest... that's my fantasy.

What is the best part of being a writer?
The phone never ringing and endless cups of coffee.

What is the worst part of being a writer?
The phone never ringing and endless cups of coffee.

LOUISE MILLAR

What kind of books do you write?
Psychological thrillers.

What did you do before you became a writer?
I worked as a magazine journalist, starting off as a sub-editor on music magazines such as *Smash Hits* and the *NME*, and ending up as a senior editor on *Marie Claire*.

What are you proudest of?
I'm proudest of Sophie Hannah picking out my debut *The Playdate* as a 'must-read', the actor John Gordon Sinclair liking *The Hidden Girl* so much he spoke about it on his own book tour, and having a nice review for *The Playdate* in the *New York Times*.

What was your inspiration for your story in this collection?

I wanted to write a story about what happens when a very lonely, vulnerable person mistakes professional care for personal intimacy and steps over the boundary. It was inspired by real-life news stories about GP-stalking, and also, as a journalist, interviewing therapists about how they are trained to deal with patients who form intense emotional attachments during therapy.

KATE RHODES

What do you write?
My crime series features the work of a forensic psychologist and is set in my home town of London. My central character, Alice Quentin, has been described by *Woman and Home* as 'a terrific new heroine on the block'.

What did you do before you became an author?
I taught English and wrote two collections of poetry, both shortlisted for the Forward Prize. I have always loved writing short stories in the intervals between novels and was lucky enough to win the Ruth Rendell prize in 2014.

What gave you the idea for this story?
My short story for this collection, 'Natural Justice' was inspired by watching crows colonising my back garden. Their stark cries, ominous black feathers and cunning teamwork made them seem like ideal characters for a murder mystery.

HELEN SMITH

What kind of books do you write?
Mysteries and thrillers.

What did you do before you became a writer?
I travelled all over the world, collecting experiences to go into my books.

What are you proudest of?
I love it when my books win awards that have been voted for by readers. The day my first book got to number one on Amazon.com was pretty exciting, too.

What was your inspiration for your story in this collection?
There is a two-hundred-year-old windmill a five-minute walk from my house in Brixton, south London. My story is set there.

LOUISE VOSS

What kind of books do you write?
I write 'domestic noir' as a solo author and a police proce-dural series (DI Lennon) with Mark Edwards, with whom I've co-written six thrillers. I also have four contemporary women's fiction titles available on Amazon.

What did you do before you became a writer?
Various things, mostly music-industry based. I've been a marketing manager for a record label in New York, a direc-tor of Sandie Shaw's company, and a concert organiser at a university. More recently I've also lectured in creative writ-ing and been a literary consultant.

What are you proudest of?
I think I'm most proud of the fact that Mark Edwards and I were the first British independent authors ever to reach number one in the UK Amazon charts. Our novel *Catch*

Your Death was on the top spot for a month in June 2011, with our other one *Killing Cupid* at number two for the same duration.

What was your inspiration for your story in this collection?
It's based on the true story of a television producer who had to undertake a road trip to retrieve a facetiously annotated reply to a viewer complaint letter that got posted in error. Needless to say that the nefarious intentions in my version of events are an entirely fictitious addition!

LAURA WILSON

What kind of books do you write?
Two different sorts: psychological stand-alones, which are mainly contemporary, and a series featuring DI Ted Stratton, which is set in the 1940s and '50s.

What did you do before you became a writer?
I grew up in a cult, did a BA and an MPhil in English Literature, and worked in publishing. All of it was useful preparation for being a writer, albeit in very different ways.

What are you proudest of?
Getting published! Also my first ever review, which was from the late Philip Oakes (*The Literary Review*). He wrote, 'In her first novel Wilson is imitating no one. She may remind you of the best, but her talent is all her own.' I was on cloud nine.

What was your inspiration for your story in this collection?
A couple of years ago I read an article about the suicide of the actor Paul Bhattacharjee, and a comment about how the acting business is not unfair, but merely indifferent, stuck in

my mind: 'It gives everything to some and nothing to others; talent, ambition and virtue have little to do with it.' It made me think more generally about how we underestimate the part that luck plays in our lives, and also about something that, in the vast panoply of self-deception, is closely allied to this – paranoia as a defence against an unpalatable truth.

If you weren't a writer, what would you be?
Assuming it's nothing to do with words, a florist or a veterinary nurse.

What is the best part of being a writer?
The simplest and best answer is that I love writing. Also, it's indoors and there's no heavy lifting.

If you've enjoyed this collection and would like to be kept in touch with future Killer Women events and publications, please sign up for our newsletter here: http://www. killerwomen.org/killer-women-club/

Printed in Great Britain
by Amazon